Reviews

'It's Our Earth Too,' written by David Still is *a captivating story full of eye opening real life content* which is cleverly displayed throughout the novel.

The author follows the lives of several characters, from their changing views on the world they live in, to surfing competitions and love interests. *I could not put this book down!* I loved the way the characters developed throughout the story and how passionate the teenagers become about their planet and the way they decide to make their voices heard by banding together.

This totally inspiring novel has left me wanting more. I can't wait for its sequel to discover how everything will unfold and what challenges the characters will face next.
Emily-May Rahmate, aged 20, Australia

I found this book to be extremely enlightening and informative yet also easy to relate to. *I definitely can't wait until book two.*
Tess McLeod, aged 16, Australia

I love the way this book has such an eclectic range of characters so that it is much more relatable to a wider audience. I personally find myself drawn to Ivy and her interest in astrology and nature spirits that you wouldn't usually read about in a book that is also educational and presses on current issues. I am excited to read book two.
Bianca Westhoff, aged 20 Australia

This book achieves a rare balance between entertainment and enlightenment. Poignant ideas and mind-blowing facts are woven seamlessly into a story of discovery, love and empowerment which will leave readers both shocked and inspired. The authenticity of the characters and the author's profound insight into humanity

keeps you captivated throughout and *leaves you desperate to read more. A true awakening for readers.*
Isabel Mackay, aged 20, Law Student, Australia

David Still's book is a standout in personal growth for young adults. This book involves and educates our young – teaching them to question, answer and act on our pressing earthly issues. It is written with youthful enthusiasm and aims comfortably as a "can't put it down enjoyable educational read." Well done David Still! At last, a life choices manual to kerb teenager apathy. *I give it 5 stars!!*
Darryn Ann Gordon, Physical Therapist,
Hypnotherapist, Psychotherapist, Australia.

Eye opening, informative and a fun read. The book is relevant and truthful, whilst not being boring. A 'must read.'
Aaron Barnes, aged 18 Australia

It's Our Earth Too is a must-read for the youth of today, many of whom feel dis-enfranchised and powerless about the mess they will be inheriting from the older generation who have been plundering the Earth's resources as if there were no tomorrow.

As well as a captivating storyline delving into the lives of a group of Australian teenagers, it addresses critical issues of the day. It demonstrates that the voice of the young is a force to be reckoned with. It shows how, rather than be swept along the path of self-destruction as the result of corporate greed and lust for power; they can assume a pro-active role and make their voice heard.

Although addressed to teenagers, the book is by no means limited to that generation but applies to everyone who draws breath on this planet and would like to continue doing so. *This is a book that offers hope to a generation facing what at times may appear to them to be a hopeless future.* Read it and share it…because sharing is what it is all about.
Jonathan Quintin, Cosmologist, New Zealand

It's Our Earth Too

Book 1: The Awakening

By DAVID STILL

IT'S OUR EARTH TOO
Book 1: The Awakening

Copyright October 2012, Evolvesmart Media Pty Limited
A.C.N. 126 850 208
www.ItsOurEarthToo.com.au

ISBN: 978-0-9874544-2-3

Cover Art by Coco Loberg www.cocoloberg.tumblr.com

This book is a fiction story and any similarities between the characters, and real persons living or dead, are unintended. The information submitted by the students in their school assignments is however real information which is in the public domain.

The Publisher and Author expressly make no representation, express or implied, about any factual matters. Information that is already in the public domain is presented in this story. For readers who wish to learn more, QR Codes are provided for quick access to further commentary on our website.

What are QR Codes?

A QR Code is a small square barcode readable by mobile phones, tablets and webcams. Once scanned by a QR Code scanner app it instantly links to a website, an address, contact info, a video, or any other web content.

If you have a smartphone all you have to do is visit your phone's app store and download a QR code reader/scanner app.

We recommend QRReader for iPhone or Android

To scan a QR code simply open the app, point the camera at the code, and you're done! There is no need to take a photo or press a button. QR Code Reader will automatically recognize any QR code your camera is pointing at. When scanning a QR code, if the code contains a website URL, you will automatically be taken to the site. If a [QR Code] or [Link] is not working directly, it can be accessed from the 'Reference Links' page of the website.

Dedication

This book is dedicated to our wonderful planet Earth, all of its amazing life, human and otherwise, and the Great Spirit that animates us all. We are all one; some of us just don't get it...*yet*.

It is also dedicated to everyone who sees the need for humanity to evolve into a more loving and cooperative team to create a better future for our children. Some have shown the way with unconditional love, others with great wisdom, and others yet with great courage and truth *(not always a good career move)*.

These courageous, honest and innovative people, past and present include Eugene F. Mallove, Brian O'Leary, Foster Gamble, Kimberly Carter Gamble, Nassim Haramein, Steven Greer, Jonathan Quintin, John Major Jenkins, David Wolfe, Paul Connett, Tom Beardon, Andrew Harms, Jack Dreyfus, Nikola Tesla, Peter Proctor, Joanna Budwig, Jacques Fresno, Ashtara, Bruce Lipton, Albert Einstein, Viktor Schauberger, Rudolph Steiner, Albert Szent-Gyorgyi, George Carlin, William Marcus, Gregg Braden, Christopher Bryson, Catherine Austin Fitts, George Walmot, Phylis Molynix, Vandana Shiva, Helena Norberg Hodge, Royal Rife, Bill Hicks, John Page, Peter Caddy, Eileen Caddy, Dorothy Maclean, Buckminster Fuller, Adam Trombly and Dane Reynolds.

You are all an inspiration to me and I hope to the next generation.

David Still
Far North Coast. NSW.
Australia

Acknowledgements

Thank you to my lovely wife Kelli for her love and support in good and tough times and for her patience and intelligent contribution to this story.

Thank you to my four wonderful teenagers for showing me how amazing the next generation are and why the world could use a book like this and especially to my amazing daughter Alanah who patiently encouraged me through the early stages of this book.

Thank you to all my wonderful friends, you enrich my time on this planet, particularly Paul for his lifelong friendship and unwavering support, Pete G for challenging me with his contrarianism, and for his wit and writing tips, Lawrie for his kindness and integrity, Darcy for his wisdom and great surfboards and Peter O (my world is not the same without you Pete).

Finally, a big thanks to my test readers, your feedback inspired me and your enthusiasm has given me great hope for the next generation.

David Still
Far North Coast, NSW,
Australia

"Treat the Earth well: it was not given to you by your parents, it was loaned to you by your children."
Ancient American Indian Proverb

About the Author

As a father of four teenagers, David believes that adults must help our younger generation to realize their unique individual value and to learn about the wisdom of nature and the true potential for humanity to flourish if they choose to. As a lifelong surfer, he is passionate about protecting our oceans and the environment generally and strongly believes our 'modern' way of life cannot be maintained.

After finishing high school David completed Bachelors of Commerce and Law and then a Masters of Laws from the University of Sydney (Australia). David then spent 8 years as a commercial lawyer and 9 years as an investment banker, including senior roles with Merrill Lynch and Goldman Sachs.

Feeling like a change from the corporate world, David retired from full-time employment in 2004 to focus, with his wife Kelli, on raising their four children on the idyllic far north coast of NSW in Australia. During this period he assisted various charities such as Australia's Disabled Surfing Association and immersed himself into learning as much as possible of the Laws of Nature and the Universe.

It's Our Earth Too is intended to entertain readers whilst gently educating them on key issues facing humanity and the great potential of every individual to make a difference. David has been delighted with the positive responses from teenage test readers, confirming his suspicion that they would naturally resonate with truth and harmony, rather than the violence, horror and celebrity worship that our media feeds them.

Table of Contents

Introduction

Cycle endings are rarely easy so why should this one be any different?

The ancients had spoken of the great alignment for thousands of years and yet the people of Earth had no real connection to what was unfolding. The masses didn't know that their planet was evolving, along with so many others in our galaxy. They didn't know of their chance to consciously evolve and unite as one. Who was going to tell them?

The Media? The Governments? Not likely.

Humans had front row seats for the greatest cycle ending in history and most of them didn't even know. What's more, many believed they were the only ones invested in the future of the Earth.

Others in our Universe had already given up on humanity. Some of us still held out hope that they would awaken. We understood the new energies that were embracing the Earth and we knew that many light workers had incarnated there to assist with the great awakening at this time.

We watched and waited, rejoicing from afar at the prospect of a harmonious Earth.

This is a story about some humans facing their potential to awaken and realize the power that lies within everyone.

Would they rise to the challenge?

THE GREAT CYCLE ENDING

1

Beauty and the beach

Crystal Stevens strode happily along the beach, a picture of youthful vitality under the warm touch of the golden morning light. Crystal's light brown hair was tied back loosely in a single ponytail and she wore a short peach coloured dress over her favourite bikini. As usual, she walked barefoot, adoring the touch of the soft sand.

'What a wonderful way to start the day,' she thought to herself, still marveling at her good fortune in landing her first teaching job in the beautiful beachside suburb of Avondale, on the east coast of Australia.

Her new home was a perfect mix of laid-back country and beachside chic, offering world-class beaches, trendy shops and cafes, and best of all, a relaxed and friendly atmosphere.

Returning to her towel, she took a sip from her water bottle and gazed out across the Pacific Ocean. Scanning the picture perfect vista she spotted a school of dolphins, her favourite of all living creatures. She watched them as they playfully frolicked, catching waves together and taking turns to leap high out of the water.

As a lone surfer shared a wave with a long line of dolphins, Crystal tried to imagine how thrilling it must be. It seemed as if the surfer and the dolphins had telepathically choreographed their rides, just as a flock of birds can coordinate in perfect formation. Crystal was thrilled and saw this as a good omen for the coming day, her first as a school teacher.

The surfer was Jay Williams, a local having his customary

early morning surf. The waves were fun and he was surfing alone, except for the dolphins. Idyllic as it was, it was the first day of a new school year and it was time for Jay to leave the water. A rare disappointment perhaps in a life summed up perfectly by his favourite saying, which was simply 'sweet.'

As Australia's best junior surfer, with Hollywood looks and a wholesome boy next door image, Jay's life really did appear to be as sweet as honey. At seventeen, he was still too young for a fulltime surfing career and so, as he told his sponsors, he would bide his time at school. Why not? He was probably paid double what a teacher earned, already, along with extra incentives for contest results and magazine photos.

Crystal watched the surfer as he walked up the beach. He appeared completely at ease, almost in a trance-like state. His brightly coloured board shorts hung loosely from his fabulous tanned physique. His wet hair was slicked back off his face, emphasizing his good looks, 'looks that certainly would not look out of place in a Calvin Klein ad,' she thought.

It appeared that the surfer had been lost in thought and then stopped suddenly as he realised he was walking straight towards someone. Crystal's emerald green eyes sparkled a warm reply to his startled gaze, until she felt like she had been staring at the surfer for long enough and quickly looked down towards the sand, her cheeks showing a slight blush.

"Did you see those dolphins?" he asked casually.

"They were amazing," she replied. "I watched you share that wave with them, it was amazing," she added, quickly making a mental note not to use the word amazing a third time in less than a minute. 'I am an English teacher' Crystal thought and this guy is hot.

"I see the dolphins most mornings," he spoke with a laid back drawl. "I swear they seem to remember me."

He stood directly in front of the morning sun and so to Crystal, he was surrounded from behind by an aura of light. The beautiful teacher and the surfer stood face to face, basking in the moment.

At just the right time the surfer broke the silence.

"They say that dolphins are smarter than we are."

"I'm sure that's true," said Crystal, confidently meeting his gaze and then adding sincerely, "just look at what we do to our planet, it wouldn't be hard."

"Hey," said the surfer, "you know Avondale means place of dolphins right?"

"I didn't," said Crystal. "I only moved here a few weeks ago. No wonder I love it," she was obviously pleased with her move.

"Welcome," he said smiling warmly, "it's a great place to live, especially in summer," he stopped and smiled and Crystal wondered what memories evoked such joy and appreciation.

"Oh well, I'd better get going. Enjoy your day," the surfer spoke in a genuine friendly tone making her feel that he was indeed sorry to leave her.

"Thanks. You too," she replied, feeling all the better for their brief encounter.

The surfer turned and ambled up the beach towards his parents' house, whistling as he went. He had to get ready for his first day as a high school senior. It would be a day of catching up with his mates and checking out the new girls in school.

Yep, life sure was sweet for Jay Williams.

2

Breakfast at Bethany's

One of the great things about Crystal's new life was living so close to the beach. It was only a short walk back to Beth's comfortable two bedroom unit and Crystal was able to stop and grab coffee and blueberry muffins on the way. She had been really lucky to see Beth's advertisement for someone to share her accommodation. The job was very much last minute but everything seemed to fall into place quickly. Best of all Crystal liked Beth immediately, they had an instant chemistry and Crystal felt blessed to have fallen into such an ideal situation.

She placed her tray on the ground and unlocked the front door to Beth's apartment. Beth was doing some stretches on the lounge room floor and was obviously pleased to see Crystal.

"Coffee," said Beth smiling broadly, "and muffins."

"Breakfast of champions," said Crystal.

"Breakfast of teachers," said Beth excitedly. "Today is your first day. How are you feeling my dear?"

"I feel great," said Crystal. "The beach was gorgeous," she added "and so was the surfer I spoke to." Crystal's eyes widened and she emphasised her message.

"*G-o-r-g-e-o-u-s.*"

This was a rarity. In the three weeks they had been living together, Beth had always been the one talking about men. Now, as they sat and ate at Beth's rustic kitchen table, the boot was on the other foot.

"Ok, I want details and I mean everything," Beth was very enthusiastic. "You know men are my favourite subject," she added as if to justify her prying.

"Well, he has a boyish smile and the abs of a Greek god," Crystal giggled and then stopped as if deep in thought, "and he loves dolphins." She pronounced this as if to complete her portrait of the perfect guy.

"Name, did you get a name?" Beth was like a detective interrogating a witness at the scene of a crime.

"I didn't Beth, but he told me he surfs with the dolphins most mornings and you know I love my morning walks," Crystal gave Beth a wink. She seemed to have it all thought out. "Now if you'll excuse me, I need to go and make myself presentable."

"Presentable," Beth scoffed sarcastically, "like, that's ever a problem for you."

Crystal thought about the day ahead as she showered and dressed. Her real concern was to connect with the kids, to be a role model and help inspire them to reach their potential. She would have to find the right balance between being too friendly and too bossy.

It was slightly weird to Crystal that she still felt and looked like a student. At age twenty-three, she was routinely asked for her identification whenever she went nightclubbing with friends. She was a little scared that the kids would not take her seriously.

3

Craig and Vanessa

Craig Sceat's mother watched him as he gazed into his bowl of cereal. He seemed to be in some kind of trance.

"Earth calling Craig," she joked. She was used to Craig. It was always a struggle to get him off to school, especially on the first day of the year.

"Sorry mum, I am on Earth, I'm just putting all my energy into dreading the day ahead." Craig put on a voice like a radio announcer and launched into a mock announcement

"Craig's prize for today is another new school, three moves in four years. Why?"

…his voice slowly falling in tone before the big finish…

"Dad's job sucks… This planet sucks."

"It's the only one we have Craig so look after it." Craig's mum had heard it all before. She was multi-tasking and seemed to be only half listening. "Vanessa," she called, "we don't want to be late on the first day."

"Ughh!" groaned Craig switching back to his announcer's voice.

"Craig's other prize is a perfect sister."

"Morning," smiled Vanessa as she breezed into the kitchen, wearing her sky blue uniform with the confidence and poise of a Paris model.

Craig loved and loathed his little sister, the fifteen year old with model looks and a free spirited personality. He knew that to Vanessa, a new school simply meant more mischief, more broken hearted boys and more jealous girls. They were opposites. Moving all the time actually suits her thought Craig jealously. How could two siblings be so different?

"I'm ready mum," said Vanessa, radiating self-confidence. Her face had a timeless symmetry, a certain golden proportion that people found interesting and attractive.

"I can't wait to meet my new classmates," she said sweetly, her perfect face breaking into a mischievous smile.

"How could anyone look forward to school?" said Craig. "Especially a new one?" he added sadly.

Yep, life sure was a drag for Craig Sceats.

4

Tommy and Tina

Tommy O'Brien whistled to himself as he made his first ever school lunch for Tina, his sixteen year old niece. It had been eight months since her mother died, and his brother Mark had been struggling as a single parent. He recently asked Tommy to live with he and Tina for a while. Tommy was pleased to be able to take some pressure off Mark. He knew his big brother's work as a lawyer was demanding and would get more so as Mark was up for a partnership this year. Money was not a problem for Mark, his problem was time.

At twenty six, Tommy was fourteen years younger than Mark. He had followed his eldest brother's footsteps to Law School. Mark's advice was a big help and they had become very close over the past eight years and especially over the last eight months.

While he was having a break from his own career, Tommy was only too happy to help Mark and especially Tina as he thought the world of her. Mark owned a big house near the beach with plenty of room for Tommy. It was a 'win win' situation, Mark could work as much as he liked and Tommy would always be around for Tina.

Tina had always been a live wire until her mum passed away. She had since become shy and introverted. Tommy hoped that the old Tina would be back again soon. Losing your mother at fifteen would be a terrible burden for any child, but for Tina, an only child of a young mother, her situation was almost unbearable. To make matters worse, her best friend Lisa had also moved away from Avondale last year.

Tommy heard Tina start the shower as he gathered the ingredients for one of his famous breakfast omelettes. 'This is going to be Tina's year' he thought to himself as he selected the ripest avocado from the bowl.

She was in Year 11 now. She was a senior.

5

Economics can be fun

Craig Sceats sat self-consciously in his first class at Avondale High. The teacher had not arrived so he doodled nervously on his exercise book, trying to avoid eye contact with the other kids as they shuffled to their seats.

The steady rabble of chatter ceased abruptly as Phil Overton strode purposefully into the room.

"Welcome to Year 11 Economics," he said with a hint of joviality. He placed his briefcase on the front desk and gave his usual opening speech about the importance of Economics. He had given this talk so many times, "Now that you are seniors, the fun will really begin. Together we will explore key concepts like marginal utility and supply and demand. It's going to be challenging but just remember," he paused as if for dramatic effect, "Economics can be fun."

Already on a roll and starting to sweat, Mr Overton walked over to turn on the ceiling fans without missing a beat in his boring speech. He outlined the assessment process and how he insisted people conduct themselves.

"Manners are important to me. I insist on being called 'Sir' at all times."

After only a few minutes, the students were glum faced, no doubt already missing last week's holiday freedom. Mike Waters, known by all as 'Super Nerd', looked like he was already regretting his subject choice. He seemed to be scanning the room somewhat suspiciously through his John Lennon glasses.

Two of the students kept glancing slyly at the ceiling fans as they slowly increased in speed. Unbeknown to all, they had arrived early and balanced some water filled balloons on the blades of the old fans with masking tape. They watched impatiently, noticing the fans getting faster and then, the first water bomb suddenly flew off the fan,.....splat! Then another, and another, three water balloons, one direct hit and quite some chaos.

Perhaps attracted to him by his negativity, the first water bomb had splattered directly onto Craig Sceats, wetting his hair, his shirt and his notebook. He was soaked and worst of all, he was the centre of attention. The self-conscious new guy was already having a bad day. It just got worse. For a moment he just sat there stunned, processing the situation.

Meanwhile Phil Overton exploded with rage.

"This is an outrageous act in my classroom. I demand to know who did this. Now is your chance to confess because rest assured, I will catch whoever did this."

He yelled at everyone, even poor Craig who made the mistake of putting up his hand and saying,

"I'm wet Sir."

This caused the whole class to laugh and make the teacher seem even madder. There was no way anyone was going to admit to anything so he simply walked out and shut the door.

Sometimes affectionately known as 'Crapper', Dane Capper was the class clown. He gazed briefly at Jay Williams, his partner in this little distraction, who gave him a quick wink. Dane also had a big heart. He took a towel from his bag and offered it to Craig as if to say I'm sorry, but without admitting anything to do with the water bombs.

"You look like you need a towel mate," Craig could see that Dane was trying not to laugh.

"Yeah thanks," said Craig as he gratefully accepted the towel, wiping his shirt and hair and mopping the water from his exercise book. The kids were all laughing, not at Craig but just at what had happened. Once he and his desk were wiped down, Craig gave Dane his towel back.

"Thanks, I really appreciate that," he said feeling extremely embarrassed.

"Welcome to Avondale High," said Dane. "Economics can be fun," he added, winking at Craig.

"Yep," said Craig, running a hand through his untidy and now wet, thick brown hair. He smiled despite his predicament. At least someone had been nice to him.

Phil Overton stormed back into the classroom holding a mop and bucket. He insisted the culprits 'own up and clean up.' Minutes ticked by and nobody owned up. It was a stand-off, surprise surprise.

Eventually, with a face like a beaten finalist, Mr Overton placed the mop and bucket down and conceded defeat, returning once again to his Economics lecture.

6

I love your country

Dane Capper spent recess with Jay and their great mate Barry Hobbs, in their usual spot just outside the canteen. They were leaning on the railing trying to look inconspicuous but cool, watching all the canteen traffic, ever alert for any pretty new students. You just never know.

Barry had moved to Australia from England a year before and although he didn't surf or skate, the boys loved him. He was a born salesman and a budding entrepreneur. He always seemed to have a hilarious story to tell and today was no exception. He was telling the boys about the recent visit his older cousin Robbie had made to Australia.

"Robbie and my oldest brother Dave were at the Marble Bar and they've met two lovely girls. Twins actually," said Barry raising his eyebrows.

"Twins," Dane and Jay repeated, clearly eager to hear the rest of the story.

Barry continued. "At closing time the twins kindly invited the boys back to their place. They'd had a lot to drink and when sly old Robbie suggested a game of strip poker, the twins agreed. They were all in their underwear laughing at Robbie as he seductively removed his boxer shorts. Suddenly the twin's parents arrived home unexpectedly."

"No way," said Dane. He and Jay were giggling as Barry continued.

"So can you imagine Robbie, drunk, naked and white as a bowl of flour? He's looked right at the twins' parents and said with great honesty

"I love your country!"

Dane and Jay roared with laughter and Barry couldn't help himself, he burst out laughing as well.

"That's crazy," laughed Jay. "Robbie is the man," he added just as the bell went for the next class.

"We'd better head off aye," said Jay.

"Relax dude, its only General Studies," said Dane. His big sister Jasmine had told him that this subject didn't really count for their Higher School Certificate.

"It was just practice at researching and writing," she had told Dane. Careful not to rush or over exert themselves, the boys casually set off for class, still laughing at Barry's story as they went.

7

Crystal's first class

Crystal Stevens had done her best to dress in a conservative way. She had chosen a plain black skirt which sat just above her knees, with a cream silk blouse and a pair of flattish shoes. Crystal wore the simple pearl earrings her parents had given her as a Graduation present and no make-up apart from lip gloss.

Despite her efforts, it was impossible to hide her beauty. Crystal had an attractive ease about her, she was comfortable in her own skin and this made people feel good around her. All eyes were on her as she marked the roll, finishing just as there was a knock on the door.

Crystal opened the door, "come in guys," she said as Dane, Jay and Barry stood there like three stunned mullets.

"I'm Miss Stevens," she said, "and you are?" She looked at them one by one so she could complete the roll and put it to one side.

"Dane Capper," said Dane as Crystal marked him off and then motioned him to the empty seats in the front of the classroom. He put his bag on his desk and rolled his eyes at Jacob Vaughan as if to say 'Whoa, how hot is this teacher?'

She turned to Barry. "Umm, Barry Hobbs," he said blankly. Barry would later say he went into shock when he saw Miss and could not remember anything.

"Jay Williams," said Jay when his turn came. "Sorry we are late

Miss," he paused with a look of recognition and then continued, "Hey, you're the dolphin lady."

Crystal smiled at Jay for the briefest moment and then she was all business. She too recognized Jay as the confident and rather attractive surfer she had spoken too that morning. His slicked wet hair was now dry and wavy and his muscled torso was now covered with a school shirt, but that smile was impossible to forget.

'Oh my god,' thought Crystal. She was surprised and embarrassed that she had looked at one of her students that way. He seemed so confident, so much older. Crystal thought about her conversation with Beth and she could feel herself blushing. She forced herself to continue.

"General Studies is all about current affairs," said Crystal. "It's about you expressing your views on current issues in our society." While Crystal knew that General Studies was not considered to be an important subject, she genuinely believed that she could make it interesting and fun. It was all about getting students to be able to present their views on a topic, something current. Rather than just hand out a list of topics, she had decided to let students choose their own topics.

"Ok here is an example straight from this morning's paper. Whether Australia should introduce a Carbon Tax? You have probably all heard about this, or heard your parents talk about it," said Crystal optimistically as she wrote this topic, with the words

For   and   **Against**

on each side of the whiteboard.

"This is a good example of a topic because it's current, and people have strong views either way. Does anyone have any thoughts?" she added, gazing hopefully around the room.

Jay Williams raised his hand and Crystal nodded to him. "Well we have to save the planet right."

As Crystal wrote the words *'Save the Planet'* under the 'For' column, Dane Capper raised his hand. "It's just a tax Miss, how will it actually help the planet? The tax on poker machines has not stopped people gambling, the tax on cigarettes has not stopped smoking, and they just raise money for the Government. The Government ends up depending on the money, it's stupid."

"Excellent," said Crystal, and as she turned to write *'Will it actually help the planet?'* A number of other hands shot up. As the other kids thought about what they could say, Dane flashed Jay a smug sideways glance, suggesting he knew Jay was just trying to impress Crystal and that he thought he had gone one better. Truth be told, Dane had impressed her by repeating what he had heard his older sister Jasmine say many times.

Unbeknown to Crystal, Jay and Dane were two of the coolest kids in the school and so their participation gave their stamp of coolness to her class. This was a lucky break, a burst of momentum for her to get the ball rolling.

One by one, with a nod from Crystal, the kids added their views. "Australia's pollution is just a small fraction of China," said Mike Waters. The Super Nerd was witnessing his dream, a situation where it was actually cool to join a class discussion. Despite being sixteen, Waters already acted like a University Professor and usually prefaced everything he said with the words 'in my opinion.'

"In my opinion," he added, "every country has to do something or it's just no use." Mike had done the math himself. He knew Australia's pollution was a drop in the bucket compared with China or India. Sometimes he wondered why things were so obvious to him, but not to other people, especially adults. He seemed quite satisfied with the point he had made.

Crystal added *'What about much Bigger Polluters'* to the Against column and the kids continued. She wished she had asked the kids to say their names before they spoke, but otherwise, she was absolutely delighted about the discussion. There was a wide variety of views, and the kids were more passionate than she expected.

Albert Rose was known and respected as a star of the school

football team. He rarely spoke in class, especially if he didn't have to. Albert was aboriginal and treasured all he had learned from his uncles on his trips back home. Stories and legends had been passed down from generation to generation through a fierce determination to keep the knowledge alive. He raised his hand to speak, perhaps feeling that it was his duty to pass on what he had heard.

After an encouraging nod from Crystal, Albert began.

"It should not be about money," he paused to let those words sink in and then continued, "the Earth is alive and all of nature is connected. If we harm the planet, we harm ourselves and our future. Indigenous people have been saying this forever and nobody listens."

The room was silent as Albert continued. "If man harms any part of nature he is harming himself because all are one. No tax is going to change this. Our elders have told this story for a long, long time. They talk about a time when humans will understand their oneness with each other and all of creation. Their hearts will open and they will embrace and respect the abundance of nature. We cannot create a world like this while we just think about money."

Crystal saw that the kids were paying very close attention to Albert, and that his words seemed to really affect them. She thanked him for the wisdom and the students for their enthusiasm. It was time to outline how they would be assessed for this subject. Crystal explained that General Studies was all about being able to research a topic and present the arguments.

"Just like our discussion on the carbon tax, you could summarise the arguments on the whiteboard and end with a conclusion about what to do."

Crystal had a lovely speaking voice and virtually had the class mesmerized. "Each of you will need to choose a topic that is current, research it and present your views to the class. Given that you are all so enthusiastic about things like pollution and politics, I would suggest a general topic like *What Would I do to save the World?* The adults aren't doing too well, maybe you kids can do better?" she teased.

Thinking about it later Crystal realized that this idea had simply come into her head without any conscious thought. She was initially delighted about this idea, seeing that by offering the kids a chance to say what they would do, she had really empowered them.

A number of hands shot up. Everyone liked the topic and the questions were mostly about the format, things like whether the presentation needed to be in writing, could it be a PowerPoint, could they use video clips.

"What about a movie?" asked Craig Sceats. He would later say that he was simply thinking out loud and had surprised himself both by talking without meaning to and by actually participating in a class discussion.

"A movie would be fine," said Crystal, "as long as you put forward your views and your conclusions." Crystal was delighted to see how well the kids were reacting to being given a choice.

"Don't forget, I am encouraging anyone who wants to creatively use new media. You can probably work that equipment much better than I can. Making a movie; that was a great suggestion by," Crystal looked at Craig who finished her sentence, "Craig."

"What about a Rap Song?" asked Dane Capper, causing some kids to burst out laughing.

"You freak," said Jay Williams, rolling his eyes to the sky. He knew his mate to be a gifted guitarist with good overall musical skills, but a rapper? No way.

"A rap song is fine too, very creative," said Crystal, admiring Dane for his ability to think outside the square.

"You would also need to hand in a summary of your views as a two page written synopsis. That will be your assignment and the rap song is a way of emphasising your conclusions." Crystal had hoped for some class participation but this was beyond her wildest dreams.

"As you all know we have General Studies twice a week and I would like to get a presentation started next week if possible. For Thursday's class, I was planning to show some movie clips on current affairs topics just to give you some ideas. If anyone wants to volunteer to do the first presentation next Monday that would be fantastic," said Crystal with a hopeful smile.

Noticing all of the kids immediately looking down at their desks, she realised her suggestion may have been a little optimistic. 'Where is my volunteer,' thought Crystal, as she gazed at the tops of her students' heads. Tick, tock, tick, tock, the silence was just becoming uncomfortable for Crystal when, for the second time that day, the voice of Jay Williams made her feel at ease.

"Miss I can do a presentation on the oceans," he said. "We really need to clean them up," he added seriously and then switched to a high mocking voice, "and don't get me started on our marine life."

Dane winced as all of the girls, who had been listening in awe, giggled at Jay's funny voice.

"Excellent," said Crystal so happy to have a volunteer that she could have given him a big hug then and there.

"Perhaps the rest of you will get some ideas from the movie clips I will show in Thursday's class." She tried to sound nonchalant but in reality she was damn proud of her first class as a teacher.

At that moment the bell went. "Thank you all for your participation," Crystal was really grateful to the kids. "I look forward to seeing you on Thursday."

Wow thought Crystal, so far so good.

8

A lunchtime chat

Craig Sceat's first day at Avondale High was like no other. He had been hit by a water bomb in Economics and then had spoken voluntarily in General Studies. Now, as he walked along the quadrangle wondering where to eat his lunch, Craig heard someone call his name. Another person wanted to talk to him, a female no less.

"Craig?" asked Tina following behind him. He stopped and turned towards her puzzled. He could only assume it was a case of mistaken identity. Like Craig, Tina was quite tall. Her dark wavy hair fell loosely across her face and as she reached him, she stopped and pulled her hair back, accentuating her large brown eyes.

Craig managed to squeak out a brief "Hi", before waiting for her to speak.

"I was in your last class, I heard you ask about making a movie, I was just about to ask the same thing." Tina continued nervously, "I want to make a movie too. Maybe you can give me some tips," she added with a shy smile which enchanted Craig.

"Sure" he said, trying not to appear as grateful as he was.

Craig and Tina chatted away like love struck teenagers. Craig explained about the family move to Avondale, but unlike that morning at breakfast, he no longer needed to say how much he thought it sucked. Tina gave him the heads up on the school, the teachers and some of the people and of course they both had a good laugh about Economics class.

"Economics can be fun," said Craig sarcastically. He felt completely at ease with Tina.

It was only the five minute warning bell that brought them back to their surrounds.

"I have maths after lunch," said Tina as their eyes briefly met. "I can't be late, I have Mr Southwell. He's pretty crazy apparently."

Craig was a new guy, he had no idea about anything but he scanned his timetable as rapidly as humanly possible. 'Maths, Mr Southwell, yes.' thought Craig, 'Yes, yes, yes, it is my lucky day.'

"Ah I've got him too," he said to Tina, trying to be nonchalant. "I'm pretty sure I'll be the one he screams at if we are late," he added and was up and ready to go in the blink of an eye.

With that, two of the shyest kids in Year 11 made their way across the quadrangle to Maths class together feeling enlivened simply by talking with each other through lunch. As they walked Craig realised that they had forgotten to even talk about making a movie.

9

Jedi mind control?

Crystal sat alone in the staffroom eating a salad sandwich. Still trying to gather her thoughts after her first class, she was high on adrenaline and quietly laughing to herself.

"Is it ok if I join you?" A fellow teacher introduced himself as Bill Edwards. He was interested to hear about Crystal's first lesson and seemed a little surprised that things had gone so well. Edwards had taught Year 10 last year and asked Crystal if she was sure she had Year 11?

"Of course Bill, Year 11 General Studies," she said. "Tell me who is in your class" he asked as if to double check. "Jay Williams, Dane Capper, Barry Hobbs....."

The three latecomers' names were enough to convince Bill Edwards.

"Stop!" he said. "You must have a guardian angel."

"Seriously Bill, the kids were really interested in the discussion, they made some great points and Jay Williams even volunteered to do the first presentation next week. I am so surprised that anyone volunteered at all," said Crystal. She was really pleased about her class and could not hide her pride.

"You know teenagers," said Bill. "If Jay does something the other kids were likely to follow him. As a first year teacher I'd say you hit the jackpot."

"I sure hope so," replied Crystal cheerily.

"So tell me Crystal, how did you get Jay to volunteer. Was it Jedi mind control?" Edwards' tone was sarcastic but friendly.

Without knowing why, Crystal immediately thought about that moment at the beach when their eyes had first met. She had been enchanted by Jay's smile and his relaxed yet confident presence. Maybe he had felt a similar attraction. Who knows? That's all academic now she thought.

She flashed a mysterious smile at her colleague, "no Jedi mind control Bill," she said sweetly.

10

Black ball in the side pocket

Dane Capper gazed along Avondale Beach scanning the waves they would soon be surfing. The view from the top floor of Jay Williams' family beachfront house was as good as they come. Jay's parents both worked an hour away in the city so the boys had their own private after school sanctuary, complete with a full size snooker table.

Dane looked back down at the table and lined up his shot.

"Blue ball in the corner pocket," he said and 'whooped' at Jay as his prediction came true. He and Jay ribbed each other playfully in their best gangster language as the game continued. Talk eventually turned to Miss Stevens and Dane gave a long whistle.

"Dude, I have *never* seen you volunteer to do schoolwork," he teasingly told his best mate. "What are you, the teacher's pet?"

"Talking about the oceans will be too easy," said Jay. "I virtually have a readymade presentation at my fingertips. You know how I spent the last few weeks travelling the Pacific with my sponsor Natural Rhythm, they had a crew who were right into that stuff, we had scientists on board, and all sorts of scientific stuff. It was all about saving the oceans."

"You didn't mention any scientists, only swimsuit models," said Dane suspiciously.

"Yes, there were swimsuit models, but we tried very hard not to let them distract us from our important work," Jay's tone sounded almost believable.

"Of course," said Dane, "and volunteering first has nothing to do with Miss Stevens being the hottest teacher ever?"

"Hottest teacher? Dude she is probably the hottest female ever, full stop," said Jay. "I saw her on the beach, remember? She is a babe, but like I said, talking about the oceans will be too easy so I just thought I'd get it over with."

"Whatever," said Dane, rolling his eyes before continuing. "Natural Rhythm might as well do your assignment, they look after everything else for you. Miss Stevens will be really pleased."

Dane lined up his shot and carefully potted the yellow ball. As he walked to have his next shot, he turned to Jay thoughtfully, "General Studies is not even serious. Let's have fun Jay, let's combine." Dane continued with his best sales pitch, "you talk about the ocean and I can do a rap song at the end."

"What are you, Capper the Rapper?" Jay was incredulous. He was trying not to laugh at his great mate.

Dane was distracted and missed his next shot. He motioned Jay to have his go. "It's only school, who cares," said Dane, continuing to state his case. "Seriously Jay, I'll do a rap song about the pollution to go with what you say. It's too easy."

"Dude you have lost your mind? Can you even rap?" Jay was understandably dubious.

"Can I rap?" Dane repeated, looking at Jay as if to say, how could you even be asking that.

"Black ball in the side pocket," said Jay as he lined up the winning shot. The black ball dropped with a familiar thud and the white ball stopped nicely out of harm's way.

"Sweet" said Jay. Dane knew Jay better than anyone. He knew that Jay loved to win. Surfing, pool, girls, it didn't matter, life was like a game and Jay Williams always seemed to make the lucky throw.

"Let's hit the waves you crazy freak rapper," said Jay as he put the cover back on his pool table.

11

Tina and Tommy

Tommy O'Brien looked up and saw Tina walking towards him.

"Hello hello," she said in a carefree voice.

"How was it Tina, day one and loads of fun?" Picking Tina up from school each day was one of Tommy's duties and he was trying to make it fun.

"It was actually …..ok," said Tina, still cautious of being too optimistic about her life.

'Wow, she seems to be in high spirits,' he thought as they drove past South Avondale Beach. It was not what he was expecting after the first day of school. Tina was quite talkative in the car and kept going when she arrived home. Tommy listened attentively as he made them both a banana and strawberry smoothie.

"You should've seen it Uncle Tommy," said Tina enthusiastically. "It was so cool and it made me think of mum. I told you what she said to me about everyone coming together without fear."

"In your dreams," he responded.

"Now you sound like dad," he could hear disappointment in her voice. "I'm sorry Tina, I know that sounded bad, I believe you and I think it's great," he added in a conciliatory tone.

"Why did it make you think of your mum?" It was pretty out there getting messages from your dead mother but Tommy could see that this was important to Tina.

"Miss Stevens asked us what would we do to save the world and straight away I thought of her." Tina paused to collect herself and then continued, "Mum said there will be a time of great change because the Earth needs it. Change is good though right, that's what mum said, like what the caterpillar calls the end, the butterfly calls a new beginning."

Tina paused to take a sip of her smoothie, and then continued.

"I can't explain, it just seemed funny that the teacher would ask US about saving the world, that's all. It just seemed to me that this is what mum was telling me about, like we all need to lose our fear, to somehow stand in OUR power."

Tommy felt a shiver down his spine. He knew his brother thought the dreams were all in Tina's head, like some sort of coping mechanism he didn't want to encourage. He knew Mark wanted Tina back to normal. Any parent would, but then again, you lose your mum at fifteen and normal goes out the window.

"I think that's great Tina. I think the world really needs to change too, I'm just not sure how." Tommy didn't know what else to say and it didn't matter as Tina suddenly changed the subject.

"Hey Uncle Tommy, you would have been proud, I introduced myself to a new boy today and had lunch with him. His name is Craig, he is really nice, he just moved here from Albury."

"Miss Stevens said we can make a movie and that is something I would love to do," said Tina, as if by way of explanation. "It was Craig's suggestion so I followed him after class. I introduced myself and we had lunch."

"Of course," said Tommy feeling mystified but delighted. "So what did the movie man say?"

"That's the funny thing," said Tina, "we didn't even discuss it over lunch. We talked about lots of other stuff. Craig is really cool Uncle Tommy, I hope you meet him soon."

Tommy noticed something different about Tina, she seemed more…carefree, yeah that's it. He was sure about it and it filled his heart with hope.

12

Dinner at Craig's

Jane Sceats lovingly served a roast dinner as her husband Bill uncorked a bottle of red wine. Bill was the blame of course, for all the moving, so Jane insisted he at least be home for dinner on the kids first day at Avondale High. Jane wanted them to deal with Craig together. As they enjoyed their meal, Bill and Jane began to pry out the details. They were all surprised to hear Craig's description of his first day.

"Great," he said, surprising even himself.

"A great first day at school?" said Bill. "Who are you and what have you done with my son?"

They all laughed and then Vanessa asked accusingly, "that wouldn't have anything to do with the girl I saw you talking to at lunchtime would it?"

Craig was surprised and a little embarrassed. Clearly there were no secrets at Avondale High School. Vanessa explained herself,

"I wanted to borrow some money from you, but when I tracked you down and saw you two, I didn't want to cramp your style. Pretty girl too," she added, sounding puzzled.

"I swear she just came over and introduced herself to me," said Craig, still in shock.

"That's my boy," said Bill.

Craig told the story of his whole day, starting with how he had been hit by a water bomb in Economics.

"It ended up being really funny, not bad at all apart from a bit of water," said Craig. "Then I had the coolest teacher in the world for General Studies. She treated us with respect and is letting us choose our own topics for our projects."

He continued, "I asked a question about making a movie, I was just thinking aloud and didn't even mean for the words to come out. Then a girl from my class followed me at lunchtime to talk about making a movie."

"Funny thing is," said Craig, "we talked all through lunch about everything except making a movie. What's happened to me?"

It had been a long while since his parents had seen him this happy.

"Maybe nerds are cool at Avondale?" suggested Vanessa cheekily.

"No, it's just lucky we both had Miss Stevens," he said.

"Miss Stevens," said Vanessa showing instant recognition. "I have her for English, she's like a supermodel."

Craig knew Vanessa was a social animal and that her radar was acutely tuned to the competition, which was basically any other pretty girls on *her* turf.

"I agree, she's beautiful and really nice as well." He made no attempt to disguise his infatuation with Crystal.

Vanessa then spoke about her day and he listened with renewed interest. She had a real eye for detail and a talent for the dramatic. She was born to be on the stage and had already been dancing and singing for many years. Vanessa kept her family entertained with some funny impressions of Avondale High, especially her new teachers.

"I told you this new school wouldn't be so bad," said Vanessa. For once, Craig had to agree with his sister's positive outlook.

13

Crystal's second class

The teachers and students of Avondale High were gradually getting back into their school routine after the long summer break. Crystal got to know her English classes and a few more of the teachers. She was enjoying her working life immensely.

Crystal's second class went just as smoothly as her first. She showed scenes from DVDs on current topical matters to get the kids thinking about their assignments. Crystal had borrowed the DVDs from her flatmate Beth who was quite alternative, and loved to talk about how the world needed change. To Crystal's surprise, she only got through three of the scenes Beth had recommended. The class was so enthusiastic in their discussions that they ran out of time.

First of all they started with *Simply Raw, Reversing Diabetes in 30 Days,* an American documentary which shows lifelong diabetics being weaned off their insulin completely, after just a few weeks of eating raw foods. This one really struck a chord with the kids because it was so real. The kids laughed as they watched the diabetics react when they were first served raw food, it was classic, they just looked at the meals as if they were from another planet.

The kids watched each participant as they realized what was happening. They were angry and so were the kids. You could see the pennies drop as each person in the movie would say things like,

'Why didn't my doctor tell me this?' and, 'Why have I been getting needles for most of my life instead of being told about nutrition?'

"Some doctors are virtually just drug dealers," said Charlotte Huntley. "They say the father of modern medicine was *Hippocrates* and his motto was *Let the Food be Your Medicine*. Since when do doctors ever ask us what we eat?"

SIMPLY RAW – REVERSING DIABETES

Gemma Healey fidgeted during this discussion and then made some notes in her exercise book. *Speak to dad re diabetes and Hippocrates. He will know.* Her father Rupert was a doctor and in her eyes he could do no wrong.

Warren Longbottom, affectionately known as 'Tubbsy' was transfixed by Raw. Each day the people in the movie took greater control of their own health and destiny, and by the second week, they were getting slimmer with each scene. Warren wasn't diabetic but he was quite overweight and the statistics said he probably would be a diabetic soon.

As Crystal finished the clip, Tubbsy spoke out to nobody in particular. "Wow that was cool, I didn't know any of that stuff, and my family don't even eat things that are not cooked."

"Tubbsy old mate, that explains a lot," said Barry Hobbs, adding, "Maybe you should borrow that movie from Miss Stevens and show your oldies."

"Yeah," Warren's chubby face broke into a broad grin, he showed no embarrassment at all.

Crystal gave the class a summary of how someone should present 'Raw' showing arguments both ways and concluding that diet should be made more important in treating diabetes, that is, it seems better than just being resigned to take insulin for the rest of your life.

"Any questions?" she asked.

LET THE FOOD BE YOUR MEDICINE

Nobody had any so Crystal continued, "Ok, it's time for the next clip, it's called Firewater." This one was about the fluoride in our water. In the scene Crystal showed, the former head of the South Australian Dental Association, Dr Andrew Harms BDS(Adel) SA said he was strongly against fluoride now that he knew the truth.

*'As soon as I realised that the fluoride added to our water supplies was actually **toxic waste**, I told everyone it has to stop.'*

Crystal had seen this before and she knew it was shocking, a senior dentist admitting that toxic waste is added to our water because it's too expensive for industrial companies to dispose of. She had a funny feeling in her stomach as she saw just how angry the kids were getting.

"Fluoride is really good for teeth," announced Gemma Healey triumphantly, as if she somehow knew a special secret that nobody else knew.

"That is totally not true Gemma you idiot," the words flew from Charlotte's mouth like bullets. "We are drinking toxic waste," she continued and then glared at Gemma.

Charlotte has suffered many cruel taunts from Gemma over the years because Charlotte's family are not as wealthy as Gemma's. Charlotte seemed pleased to finally have the shoe on the other foot, maintaining her superior look as Gemma went bright red.

The class had a heated discussion about fluoride until Crystal said it was time to move on. The underlying theme of both clips so far was that things were not what they seemed. Maybe the Government was somehow misleading us all.

FIREWATER: AUSTRALIA'S FLUORIDATION DISGRACE

Crystal felt a little uneasy at the kids' anger. She wasn't trying to start a revolution, she just wanted them to learn to think for themselves.

Crystal decided then and there to change the mood. It was time for a laugh. Whilst she chose a clip from *The Great Global Warming Swindle,* which basically says global warming is all made up, she opted for something light hearted. Instead of showing the scientists criticizing global warming, Crystal chose the scene where scientists in all shapes and sizes explain what actually determines our temperature. It's the sun they said, not carbon. Boy were they ever sarcastic, making it sound like a complete surprise, saying things like:

'You know what actually determines our temperature? Yep, it's actually that big yellow round thing in the sky.'

The scientists thought this was really funny and the kids all laughed and so did Crystal.

"Miss, I know how to make the world a better place, I mean, I know what I want to talk about."

THE GREAT GLOBAL WARMING SWINDLE

Ivy Watkins was a gentle soul, a vegetarian who could see things most others couldn't, like fairies and nature spirits. Ivy seemed to love animals and nature a lot more than people. She had an innocence about her that was engaging. Lots of the boys had secret crushes on her.

"I saw 'The Cove,' a documentary on slaughter of dolphins in Japan." She stopped as if feeling the suffering of every dolphin. "I'll do my assignment on stopping animal cruelty," she added with conviction and this was no surprise to anyone who knew her.

"Good for you Ivy," said Crystal, seeing her passion and wanting to acknowledge it. "Jay is presenting on Monday, and Thursday is the Swimming Carnival, so the next spot would be Monday week," said Crystal.

"Ok miss, I will do it then," said Ivy.

Perhaps so as not to bow out of the race for Miss Stevens' attention, Dane Capper raised his hand. "Miss, I can do the next available spot after Ivy."

"Ok, that's great thanks Dane."

Crystal was thrilled, her General Studies class was her favourite because the kids were all so interested in what they were doing. It was a lot more fun and relevant than teaching Shakespeare.

14

Coffee and wisdom

Tommy O'Brien stared at his laptop computer hoping some inspiration would jump out at him. He was at an impasse, gun shy, scared to pull the trigger on his new venture. Losing his job unexpectedly had been a real blow and he felt totally lost.

He was a lawyer just like his brother Mark. Unlike his more sensible older brother, Tommy just scraped through University, too much partying and not enough hard work. His grades were average and it was becoming apparent to him that he was really just making up the numbers at job interviews and law firm open days.

That was until lady luck smiled Tommy's way. His charisma and enthusiasm during an interview had impressed the Managing Partner of Mason & Gordon, a prestigious law firm. John Mason was an excellent person to impress.

Tommy was hired in the firm's Commercial Department and worked very hard to build his name over the next few years. He got on well with clients and he liked his job. He was moving up the ladder and he was delighted at how rapidly his salary was increasing.

He had been at Mason & Gordon almost four years when he met Heidi. Heidi was a 'Christmas Beetle,' the name lawyers give to the handful of final year law students working at the big law firms during their last University summer vacation. Summer spots are very hard to get, and it was John Mason no less, who had invited her to the firm as a favour to his son David. Although it wasn't known throughout the firm, Heidi had been David's girlfriend for the last three years and so John ensured she was hired.

Any summer student was strictly off limits socially and Tommy was smart enough to know this. He supervised Heidi's work on a Trust Law matter and they had four meetings together. He found her bright and engaging and they got on really well. To his credit Tommy remained businesslike at all times and would look away when Heidi had tried to hold his gaze.

The Firm's Christmas Party was a test for Tommy's resolve. After a long party, some heartier souls continued on to Players Nightclub for more dancing and drinks. It was very late when Heidi made her move. She asked Tommy for a dance and as they danced, Heidi made it clear to Tommy that she 'liked' him. She met Tommy's glance and when Tommy suggested that hooking up would be strictly taboo, Heidi assured him that she could definitely keep a secret.

Tall, blonde, athletic and with a vivacious personality, she was definitely attractive to Tommy and in his drunken haze, he was aching to hold her. As she danced seductively before him, the illogical part of his brain was quickly convincing the logical part of his brain that nobody would ever be the wiser. Tommy was at least smart enough to suggest that they leave separately and discreetly meet downstairs, which they did.

It is probably fair to say that if not for his secretary Kim, Tommy and Heidi would never have been noticed. Kim had been working for Tommy for two months and flirting with him whenever she could. Tommy hadn't realised that she was watching as he danced with Heidi.

Not known for her discretion, Kim confronted Heidi at work the next morning and tricked her into admitting she had been with Tommy. Embittered by her jealously, Kim spread the word around the office and by mid-morning, Tommy and Heidi were the latest scandal at Mason & Gordon.

Many firms ignore such behaviour if it doesn't actually affect their reputation. It's like an exclusive club willing to accept bad behaviour from members provided they make lots of money for the firm. Tommy was an excellent biller and would have been safe except for one small detail. John Mason felt embarrassed for his son.

"What do you have to say for yourself Tommy?"

Tommy decided to be honest and up front.

"She's not a child John, she's 21 you know."

John seemed to ignore Tommy's comment.

"The thing is Tommy, I feel that I have let David down."

"David who?" asked Tommy, genuinely puzzled.

John was clearly angry.

"My son David! After all, Heidi is his girlfriend and I invited her here."

Tommy knew that with this last piece of information, things had definitely taken a turn for the worst. All he could think of was, 'Heidi, that is not a good detail to leave out,' as he tried not to look as horrified as he felt.

"I'm really sorry John, it was a serious error. I will apologise to David if you like. I obviously had no idea." Tommy knew he was in the wrong and wanted to fix it and move on.

John Mason's eyes were cold and unfeeling.

"Tommy, I don't think you understand, today is your last day at Mason & Gordon. You have one hour to pack up and leave."

Tommy felt a lump in his throat and tears in his eyes. He was too shocked to speak. True to his word, John came back one hour later and escorted Tommy down in the elevator.

"You'll stay away from Heidi if you know what's good for you."

Those were his mentor's parting words.

Tommy went through an intense period of self-loathing and he wished he could have that night all over again. To make it worse, Heidi had been embarrassed by all of the gossip and now wanted nothing more to do with him.

Over time he began to feel a little better and convinced himself that he would eventually get another legal job. In the meantime, he decided that he would make his living from trading on the stock market. Why? Simple. He had plenty of savings and it seemed an easy way to earn a living, with the flexibility to help Mark with Tina.

"You will do well Tommy, I'm certain." Mark had encouraged Tommy and even contributed half of the money for his new venture. They had $100,000 as capital and in the month or so since he started, Tommy still hadn't done a thing. He had definitely realised that it was easier said than done. With Mark's words ringing in his ears he would sit in front of his laptop in a variety of places, each as uninspiring as the last. It was as if Tommy had stage fright.

On this particular day, he was sitting in a booth at Cafe Destiny, waiting for Divine Inspiration. As he sipped his caramel latte and gazed absentmindedly out the front door, the most beautiful woman he had ever seen walked into the cafe.

Tommy felt as if he knew this mysterious beauty and he simply could not take his eyes off her as she and her friend walked up to the counter to place their orders.

Tommy had never been so enchanted by a woman. He was trying to remember where he knew her from. Was she famous? Perhaps on TV?

After a few minutes, he summoned the courage to approach this wonderful alluring creature. He didn't really have a plan, he simply walked over and ordered a coffee.

"Ooh another coffee," said the barista in a shrill voice to everybody listening. 'Great,' thought Tommy, blushing as he stood just across from the girls. He felt foolish and had no idea what to say.

Tommy was just about to make his move when the girl of his dreams moved first. She indicated to her friend that she had to take a call, holding up her vibrating cell phone. She turned and via one handed sign language asked her friend to grab her coffee and bring it outside. Tommy had been sidestepped like an old slow fullback.

He quickly regrouped and gave her friend a warm smile but she simply grabbed their coffees and walked out the door. The girl of his dreams had just walked into his life and straight back out in quick succession. Tommy stood there flustered and then grabbed his drink and turned to walk back to his booth.

The man in the booth next door gave Tommy a wry smile. He had obviously been watching.

"Not one of my smoother moments," Tommy felt embarrassed.

"No, I guess not," said the stranger.

"I'll probably never see her again," shrugged Tommy.

"If you think so?" said the stranger, in a manner which suggested that it was really all up to Tommy.

"Well, I........." Tommy looked confused as the stranger held out his hand. "Tommy," he said holding out his hand to reciprocate.

"Pleased to meet you Tommy," the stranger said slowly. "My name is Elliott."

He looked and sounded a little different to other folks, like he had come from another world to observe the strange habits of earthlings.

He held Tommy's gaze with a sparkle in his dark brown eyes, smiling warmly and motioning Tommy to have a seat.

"So what is it that you do Tommy, apart from trying to pick up girls in coffee shops?"

"I never pick up girls in coffee shops," said Tommy defensively. "I just really felt like I knew her, I...."

Tommy stopped talking. It was as if Elliott had kindly sent him his thoughts and he'd had a sudden realization that Elliott was more interested in his work than the mystery girl, so he changed his focus.

"I'm between jobs, trying to make a living trading the stock market. Something different," added Tommy, as if to explain.

"I don't know how you guys do it," said Elliott, continuing as Tommy sipped thoughtfully on his coffee. "Everyone's watching the market. Is it going up or is it going down?"

"Funny you say that, I can't actually make up my mind," replied Tommy.

"Tommy, do you value yourself the same, rich or poor?" asked Elliott, suddenly adopting a new intensity, his eyes piercing Tommy to the core. 'This guy certainly is different,' thought Tommy, as he pondered over the question.

"Yeah, yes, I do value myself the same rich or poor. Money is just money, right?" He looked at Elliott for agreement and his enigmatic response did not disappoint.

"You are blessed to have this understanding Tommy, because many in this world don't. You are coming from a place of balance and that is a good thing," said Elliott, again sounding 'other worldly.'

"So why am I so uncertain?" shrugged Tommy, before continuing.

"The brokers are saying that the market will keep going up but me I'm not sure. It can't go up forever?"

It was both a statement and a question.

Elliott spoke kindly but firmly. "Tommy you are lost because you are in conflict between your own instincts and what others are saying. You must be," he continued. "Why else would you be asking an old guy in a coffee shop about this?"

He looked right at Tommy as he continued, "Don't give away your power. Listen to your own instincts, that's why you have them in the first place."

"Well actually," said Tommy, "I do think things will crash ...but."

"Don't say 'but' Tommy, just go with your instincts." Elliot spoke with such authority, it seemed impossible to even doubt his words.

"What about the girl?" Tommy asked. "I didn't even get her name."

Elliot responded dismissively, as if Tommy was raising the simplest of problems.

"Tommy, just thank the Universe for sending her to you, sincerely, then simply act like you will see her again and you will."

Tommy was impressed, "How long will it take?"

"How long do you want it to take?" replied Elliott. "You've

got the power Tommy, don't ever forget that. Oh and as for the market, I'm with you Tommy, its heading south." He gave Tommy a knowing wink, like he surely knew something that Tommy didn't.

Tommy sat back down in his booth. It was 3.00 pm, still thirty minutes before he had to meet Tina. What the heck, it was suddenly so clear, he decided to follow Elliot's advice, in a hurry. Tommy decided to bet a big chunk of their money on a big market fall.

Tommy knew he needed *put options* over a wide range of shares. Banks, mining companies, airlines, he didn't care. He made notes as he went listing all of the cheapest put options he could find. He knew the price of put options would rise if the shares go down. In other words, Tommy was betting that the market would drop, or *head south*, as Elliott had suggested.

Once Tommy was ready, he looked up but Elliott was nowhere to be seen. He was sweating profusely as he quickly entered his trading codes into his laptop. Within twenty or so minutes, he and Mark were proud owners of a truckload of put option contracts. He felt a surge of adrenalin, like he was standing atop his own personal Mt Everest.

His stage fright was long gone. In fact, somewhat impulsively, he had just spent around half of their $100,000 kitty. 'What a rush' he thought to himself feeling totally alive. He logged off and set out towards Tina's school.

As he pulled up at the school, Tommy saw that Tina had a friend with her. 'This must be Craig,' he thought, shrewdly deciding he would say nothing to suggest that Tina had ever mentioned him.

"Hey Uncle Tommy this is Craig." Tommy held out his hand and gave Craig a welcoming smile. "Hey, I'm Tommy." "Nice to meet you Tommy," said Craig enthusiastically returning Tommy's handshake.

Tina explained, "Craig is coming over to our place so we can work on some homework together." To Tommy's credit, he acted totally normal, as if Tina always invites guys home from school.

The O'Brien family home was a beautiful house in exclusive South Avondale. With Mark as a lawyer and Christine as a doctor, the family had earned plenty of money.

As Tommy prepared a banana smoothie for each of them, Tina explained to Tommy that Craig was new to the area and that they were both interested in making a movie for the General Studies assignment.

"A movie, wow, things have certainly changed since I was in school," said Tommy. Tina explained that Tommy and her dad Mark had both been students at Avondale High.

'Class of 2003' said Tommy, who could not resist breaking into the school song.

"So Tommy how was your day?" asked Tina, slightly embarrassed about his singing and happy to change the subject.

"I actually saw the girl of my dreams today Tina, in the coffee shop and," Tommy paused thinking how best to put it.

"And," Tina prompted him. "What happened?"

"Nothing," said Tommy. "I didn't even get her name," he added forlornly.

"Ouch," joked Craig.

"In fact," said Tommy sounding deflated, "it's quite possible that she didn't even see me at all."

Tommy started singing, holding a banana as a pretend microphone

"We'll meet again, don't know where, don't know when, I'm sure we'll meet again my mystery girl."

Tina and Craig burst out laughing and so did Tommy.

"That's so sad Uncle Tommy." Tina was still a little surprised about Tommy's story, he didn't usually strike out. In fact, Tina had heard her parents say that girls just fell at Tommy's feet. It was O'Brien family folklore.

"It's all good. I'm going to head down to the beach for a run and a swim" said Tommy. He turned back towards them adding mischievously, "you two have fun now."

15

Tina's Dreams

Craig sat on Tina's comfortable leather lounge, scanning the view and waiting for her to explain why she had approached him after their first class; it was after all, highly unusual.

"How can I explain this Craig." As Tina tapped her fingers on the arm rest of her chair, she continued, "for me the first General Studies class was a surreal experience. I was captivated by Miss Stevens, I felt a strong respect for her, and I knew instinctively that her words tied in to my dreams."

Craig was curious to know more, his head rested on his hand. "Dreams?" he asked simply.

"Dreams where I spoke to the spirit of my mother, who died last year, or rather, she spoke to me. There, I've said it, you probably think I am weird." Tina seemed relieved to have gotten this off her chest.

"I'm sorry to hear about your mother Tina, but you are definitely talking to the right guy." Tina looked puzzled. "What I mean is, people always think I'm weird," said Craig, "well, I am, but so are you."

Tina still looked puzzled. "Tina, we all travel through the spirit world in our dreams."

Craig suddenly turned serious, "I do it in my dreams, so do you, it's just that some people can remember it and some can't. The ones who can't remember say we're weird."

He could have said more but he decided he wouldn't for now. "Tina, I totally believe what you are saying," he stopped and waited for her to continue.

Tina was clearly pleased that Craig understood, she paused to collect her thoughts. "Mum appears as she always looked except she is 'lighter' and even more beautiful."

Tina smiled at the thought and then looked Craig in the eye. "When she looked at me, I swear that I could feel all of the love in the Universe, and she said to me:

> *'You are part of my soul family and we agreed to help the Earth at this time of great change.'*

"It scared me at first and like totally blew my dad's mind when I told him."

Craig loved the facial expressions Tina made when she spoke. "Mum came again and again and she made me understand. You know she told me her body was no longer her 'vehicle.' She said:

> *'My life as Christine was one of many lives. I am fine now Tina, please do not feel sad for me, birth and death are short steps in our soul's journey.*

She also said that:

> *What the caterpillar calls the end, the butterfly calls a new beginning.'*

"Mum also told me about the prophecy for peace on Earth. The thing is Craig, she even said that teenagers can help bring these changes to the Earth, but only if they know about it. That's why I spoke to you."

"Lucky you did," Craig answered enthusiastically and then mentally scolded himself as Vanessa, the expert in such matters, had always told him not to appear too eager.

As Tina spoke about what her mum had told her Craig made some notes:

Movie Ideas February 2012
We are all just spirits having a human experience.
The earth is a living being and is itself evolving. We can tune in to these changes by opening our hearts and anchoring 'oneness' onto the planet.
The future on Earth is all about humans working together with other humans and nature.
The vibration of cooperation, rather than competition, is coming at the time of the great alignment.
Time is critical now. The end of illusion is fast approaching.
Do not be burdened by this, have fun, as all teenagers should.

Tina captivated Craig as she spoke and finally he couldn't listen any longer.

"Tina this is so amazing. I swear I am into all things paranormal, it's like my biggest obsession." He laughed again, "It's so funny you picked me."

"Anyone else would have laughed" said Tina. Craig chuckled, he had put up with it for years, people who couldn't understand how magic works simply couldn't accept it.

For Craig it was very easy to explain. "There are a range of frequencies people can see or hear, but really, people only see and hear a small part of what's out there. Some can hear or see a little more, like clairvoyants or people who can see auras. That's just the way things work," Craig could sense Tina's relief at his words.

"Tina, I know a lot about reincarnation, I think I've had many lives and sometimes I get weird flashbacks, let me tell you the story of eleven year old James Linegar." Craig was obviously enthusiastic about this story so Tina tucked her legs up on the lounge and got comfortable.

"As a toddler James was fascinated by World War II fighter planes. He had terrible nightmares and drew graphic pictures of planes being shot down. He told his parents that he was the pilot of the shot plane and when they asked him who shot down his plane, he looked at them as if they were simple. "The Japanese" he told them. He said his boat was Natoma and when the crew of HMAS Natoma were actually tracked down by his parents; James could name them all by sight, despite being almost 50 years younger.

There was no doubt James' last incarnation was as their ex squadron member who had been shot down, he too was named James. James Houston. Young James' stories of the crash perfectly described what the other crew members had seen the night Older James was shot down. According to his parents, young James later had an 'emotional release' when he finally went to the actual site of the crash. His parent's said it's like he just had to let it all go, and now he is no longer obsessive about fighter planes.

Young James talked to Older James' sister, who was now really old. He mentioned paintings their mother did for each of them when they were young. She was clearly shocked at what this boy said to her and had no doubts this was a real reincarnation of her dead brother."

Craig paused, "You know what Tina? This kid says reincarnation is one of life's most simple truths, and he is here to help others learn this. He is only eleven."

"That is too amazing," said Tina. "My mum told me that her contract was to leave when she did and that my dad's *contract* was to bring me up without her."

Tina stopped for a moment, it seemed to Craig that she was suddenly feeling concerned about how much she had told him.

"Craig, please remember that I haven't told anyone about this except Tommy and my dad, so please don't tell anyone."

Craig was a sensitive guy and was quite overcome with emotion about all that Tina had told him. He simply took a deep breath, grabbed Tina's hands and looked right at her,

THE REINCARNATION OF JAMES LINEGAR

"You can trust me Tina, I promise. I mean who would I tell, I'm just a new guy?" "Hey new guy," she said with a mischievous grin, "maybe you could have dinner with us?"

"Yeah I'd like that. Can I just use your phone and I'll call my mum and see."

Tina wrote a note on the kitchen bench *Craig is staying for dinner [she drew a smiley face as well]* and they went back into her study to continue their research. They ended up finding out lots of information about the New Earth and the coming changes which they discovered were foretold by ancient societies such as the Hopi Indians and Mayans.

Those same ancient societies came up again when they researched about the earth being a living being. They had understood this fact which modern people seem to have forgotten.

Craig suddenly looked up, as if having a moment of realization. "So Tina, your mum is saying exactly what the ancients said. It's like she is reminding you, us, of timeless wisdom."

They printed out a whole bunch of documents and Tina photocopied these in her dad's office. It had been a pretty intense afternoon and Tina thought they should lighten up a bit before dinner.

"Hey Craig," she said, "do you like table tennis?"

"Yeah sure." Tina could be offering some sort of punishment and Craig would still say yes.

THAT'S A SMALL PART OF WHAT'S OUT THERE

"Follow me," said Tina, who then grabbed Craig's hand and led him downstairs to the games room.

As they played, Tommy ordered takeaway pizza and arranged for Mark to collect it on the way home. By the time the four of them sat down, Craig was quite hungry. He was warmly greeted by Tina's dad Mark and felt really at home in their house.

Tommy had Craig and Tina laughing again as he told Mark his sad tale about the mystery girl. It was a bewildering story, nothing happened, but Tommy seemed obsessed by it and he was happy for everyone to laugh at his expense.

Once they finished their meal, they said their goodbyes and Mark gave Craig a lift home. When he arrived home, Craig opened the front door and saw his parents and Vanessa watching something on TV.

"Hi guys," he said trying to act as if tonight was nothing unusual. He wanted to shout it out loud, 'Tina's weird like me,' but he resisted the urge.

"I'm going to go straight up and continue with my work," said Craig. "Goodnight."

His family wanted to hear all about his night but they knew not to get in his way when he was fascinated by something (as he called it), or obsessing (as Vanessa called it).

Craig sat flicking through the materials they had copied. He pondered what Tina's mum had told her and his mind raced with possibilities. He initially googled 'opening our hearts' and from then on he was totally absorbed. Craig had pulled together lots of articles and videos about things that were on his list. Tina's mum had stressed the importance of 2012 and there was certainly lots of stuff on this.

Some websites quote ancient people as saying the world was going to end in 2012 but Craig could not find any actual evidence of this. What they said was that 2012 is more about 'evolution' than destruction. It's a chance for humanity to 'grow up', a chance for a new beginning if they take it. This view felt right to Craig. Somewhere deep inside him he felt this to be truth.

He yawned and then looked at his watch, 11.11 pm. Wow he thought, that's pretty late on a school night. He quickly saved his work and shut down his computer. Later in bed, he was still wide awake and running through his day. Deep down Craig understood exactly what Tina's mum had told her. He felt familiarity with it and that intrigued him and even scared him a little.

Tina also intrigued him just by spending time with him, when no other girls would. Craig let out a sigh of contentment.

Maybe life doesn't suck he thought as he drifted off to sleep.

16

Mark and Tommy

Tommy was reading when Mark arrived home from giving Craig a lift.

"So you finally did some trading, can I check out what you bought?" he asked Tommy.

After carefully scanning the options they now owned, he turned to his brother and said, "do you know why these options were so cheap?"

"Because most people think the market will keep going up," said Tommy triumphantly.

"That accounts for some of the cost," said Mark "but really? The reason they are so cheap is because they are all short dated which means they are just about to expire. Tommy, you are aware I take it that if they expire, we get *nothing* back," Mark's tone was curt.

Tommy explained his conversation with Elliott. "I had to act quickly." Tommy felt proud of his action.

"I had to follow my own instincts."

Mark turned and looked right at him with an unmistakable look of disgust. "You know you probably should have asked my opinion before betting the farm. I reckon you've just burnt fifty grand you idiot." He got up in a huff and walked out, catching himself just before slamming the door.

Later that night, Tommy lay on his bed replaying his conversation with Elliott over and over in his head. He'd seemed certain that everything would work out well for Tommy.

Even though he was disappointed at making Mark angry, Tommy shared Elliott's optimism. He thanked the Universe for the options and for sending him the mystery girl and then, after imaging them being reacquainted soon, he drifted off into a lovely contented sleep.

17

Mark and Tommy again

Tommy was in a deep sleep when Mark knocked firmly on his door. "Wake up Tommy," yelled Mark.

"You have got to see this."

Tommy looked at his clock, it was just after 6.00am. "Come in," he said sleepily.

Mark burst into the room enthusiastically. "Greece has defaulted on its debt, Portugal looks like it will too," he said. "World stock markets have crashed overnight."

Mark was babbling like a madman. He stopped and looked at his younger brother.

"How did you do this?" What puzzled Mark was just how perfect Tommy's trades were. The market had done exactly what Tommy had predicted.

Mark had been very angry the night before, berating Tommy for making such a daring bet. Now, because of the bad news from Europe, Mark was smiling broadly. Tommy's grin grew wider as he realised the implications of what his big brother was saying.

"Thank you Elliott," was all he could manage.

"That's it, I'm calling in sick. We have to do this Tommy," Mark sounded as if he was getting ready to go to war.

"We have got to make the most of this situation you have created baby brother." I'll even cook you breakfast ok." Mark chuckled as he turned to leave, tip toeing quietly past Tina's room. She was not an early riser.

Later that morning, after Tina had left for school, Mark and Tommy sat glued to Tommy's computer screen. Tommy was in the driver's seat but Mark was watching him very closely.

The Australian market would open shortly. The pre-market quotes said it all, a big fall was already factored into the prices. It was something like the end of the world in stock market terms.

It was a nightmare for most investors, but not for two brothers, with 'put options' galore. They were salivating at the prospect of some market carnage because they were betting on a fall in the market. Tommy thought about Elliot's words

'As for the market, I'm with you Tommy, it's heading south.'

Elliott had spoken as if he already knew and he even gave Tommy a knowing wink.

Tommy knew they were looking good. He knew that the institutional investors would want put options to protect themselves in case things got even uglier. The prices were already moving strongly and as he entered the current option prices into his spreadsheet, he stopped, a little confused.

"What the?"

Tommy needed to be sure, so he quickly checked to see if he had his decimal points in the right place. He double checked the option codes off against the current pre-open bids.

"You won't believe this," he said, looking at Mark with utter disbelief.

"The total value of our options in the pre-market is over seven million dollars."

"Show me," said Mark, almost pushing Tommy over in his eagerness to check for himself.

Tommy felt his senses heightened, he was in the moment running on adrenalin. He tried to approach the situation calmly and rationally.

"Look, I think the market will crap itself at first and maybe stabilize a bit later. Let's sell the lot," Tommy suggested, "let's sell the whole damn lot."

Mark could hardly contain his smile and it was hard to concentrate with the markets chopping and changing. "I agree," said Mark, "let's take the cash. The fear will cause a big drop as people who are forced to sell get murdered."

They worked through the list very carefully, with Tommy meticulously entering the sale prices into his spread sheet. Things were getting worse as they sold and by 10.30 a.m. the proceeds of their sales contracts stood at $10, 044,525.

Using the power of leverage and perhaps even 'blind faith' in Elliott's confidence, Tommy had multiplied their money by over two hundred times in less than twenty four hours. They sat together in stunned silence.

"It's like you put all our money on a three legged horse and it won," said Mark.

"Tommy, I have to be honest," he continued, "I mainly invested to help you get set up and to keep an eye on you. I cannot believe what has happened. You have changed our lives in an instant. I made more money today than in all my years of working hard as a lawyer."

"It's not me," said Tommy. "It's Divine Intervention.....dude you know it."

"I say intuition," said Mark. Tommy knew he had been down on anything divine since losing Christine, he was still wounded and simply wouldn't hear of it.

"You said yourself you had to follow your instincts," Mark added.

"Well whatever" said Tommy. "The fact is, without Elliot, I would not have done the trades. Face it Mark, it's like a miracle."

"Whew!!" Tommy screamed with joy.

"I'm gonna use this money to help the world," said Tommy with truly noble intentions, and he meant every word he said.

Over the next hour the newly enriched brothers had a good laugh and cry as they talked about their good fortune, about Christine and Tina, and how they would come out and face the new world as newly made millionaires.

18

General Studies: JAY TALKS ABOUT THE OCEAN

As a modern day professional surfer, Jay Williams had to be tech savvy. He sometimes edited his own surfing film clips and had his own blog to inform his fans of what he was up to. He had his own filmer, and liked to keep putting fresh surfing footage on his website. His blog had lots of followers in Australia and the many countries he had already visited around the world.

It had been easy for Jay to prepare a PowerPoint presentation using information from his sponsor. His team manager seemed really pleased when Jay had told him that his recent trip had really opened his eyes and he wanted to present this information as part of a school project.

Sponsorship these days was not just about surfing performance, it was also about character. Surf companies liked people who were unique individuals that people liked to follow. This was certainly the case with Jay. He had that X factor, a cool personality. His massive raw talent and clean cut good looks were also big plusses.

He had agreed to let Dane do the rap song as part of his presentation and even offered to do it with him. "Whatever, it'll be a laugh for sure," said Jay with true light-hearted indifference.

As far as the rap song went, Dane had spent an hour with him going through his presentation and then come back a few nights later and performed a rap song which was pretty good.

NORTH PACIFIC GYRE

And so it was, that Jay Williams stood confidently before his Year 11 General Studies class presenting a PowerPoint presentation on Pollution in our Oceans. People were shocked to see the graphic photos of the pollution in our ocean and rivers.

Like Jay, until a few weeks ago, his class mates and his stunning new teacher, knew nothing of the *North Pacific gyre*. The gyre is an island of plastic the size of Texas which is sitting in the middle of the North Pacific Ocean. The currents flow in a spiral and as they get to the centre they deposit the plastic onto this ever increasing island.

Jay's presentation had great information and graphic photos. He was able to speak about damage to coral reefs with real authority, having viewed the damage in person on his recent trip.

Crystal could see that Jay's classmates were stunned by this information, and so was she.

A born showman, Jay revelled in the limelight, and invited audience participation by asking if anyone had suggestions about how to fix this problem. When nobody volunteered a solution, Jay turned serious and said to the class,

"When was the last time you threw away a plastic water bottle?"

The class unanimously agreed that plastic bottles would need to be stamped out. With assistance from Crystal, Jay led a great class discussion. He got the class to stop and ponder the question:

How could there be an island of plastic in the ocean, so big, and yet, how come nobody knew about this?

"It's not what they tell you, it's what they *don't* tell you," said Jay. He had his audience wrapped around his little finger and he was enjoying himself. With ten minutes to go, Jay informed the class that they were in for a real treat.

"I'm pretty shocked about it, but this freak has actually come up with a pretty good rap song," said Jay.

With that Capper jumped up and organized his microphone and tape player.

"Yo what's up Avondale we gotta spread this message now," said Capper in his best fake rock star voice. Jay had also agreed to sing the chorus with Dane, and he also wore a baseball cap from his main sponsor 'Natural Rhythm', on backwards of course, for true rapper style. Capper had recorded a backing tape and Jay had organised an edited version of the pictures in his PowerPoint to be played as background.

The results stunned Crystal. It was a highly entertaining song with relevant lyrics and a good beat. The theme was clear from the chorus, teenagers needed to act now as most adults had fallen asleep at the wheel. The chorus went like this,

> *"Planet Earth it's a Garden of Eden*
> *It won't be for long because of whose leadin*
> *The younger generation have to unite*
> *Because the older generation just can't get it right."*

Kids were laughing with delight, tapping along with Dane and Jay. When the boys finished, the class erupted into applause. As Crystal thanked the boys, she could not hide her admiration for what they had done. What a team. What a song. The class was blown away. Jay had really set the bar high for the others.

Crystal needed to sit down, as she was feeling quite emotional about what had happened. As students began to head out for lunch, Hobbsy came over and high fived Jay and Dane.

"You boys were on fire," he told them, not mentioning that he had filmed the whole thing on his IPhone.

"The younger generation have to unite because the older generation just can't get it right. It rhymes and it's true. Nice one Capper. I'm lost for words mate." Barry was obviously impressed.

"So am I," said Crystal as she walked over to them.

"Thanks again Jay and Dane, that song got your message across brilliantly and Jay, your presentation was interesting and entertaining."

During lunch, Crystal did not say much, she simply sat and tried not to smile too much while listening to the other teachers swapping complaints about their classes.

DANE'S RAP SONG

19

Dinner at Gemma's Place

At dinner that night Gemma Healey asked, "Hey dad, do you know much about diabetes?"

Rupert Healey absolutely idolized his only child and he responded lovingly to her question, "well I know that it's an epidemic darling, I know the number of people with diabetes has tripled in the last 10 years".

"So dad what do you do when someone has it?' Gemma's mum was pleased to see her taking an interest in her dad's work and was quite mystified when things took a turn for the worst.

"We work out what type of diabetes it is and prescribe their medicine accordingly." Rupert continued self-importantly, "why darling, does one of your friends have it? Once they do, it's for life you know."

Gemma was not so sure about this after Miss Stevens' class.

"What about their food, can't that help them get better?" It was a fair question from a curious teenager but Rupert didn't see it that way.

"What you eat can help you avoid diabetes but once you have it, you need medicine. Food isn't medicine Gemma, it's not scientific." Rupert spoke in a patronizing tone and Gemma was confused.

"But dad, what about Hippocrees?"

"Hippocrates?" said Rupert, starting to look puzzled. "The oath all doctors take is named after him."

"That's him dad." Gemma seemed pleased they were getting

somewhere, "Didn't he say something like our food should be our medicine?" she said this with relief, as if this finally made her point obvious.

"Hippocrates was an ancient Greek, I just don't think they had diabetes back then," said Rupert dismissively. "Medicine is a lot more scientific today."

"Why the sudden interest in medicine, princess?" Mrs Healey called Gemma that when she was nervous. She knew from experience that her dear Rupert was 'one-eyed' when it came to medicine. It was his way or the highway, and accordingly, Mrs Healey was nervous about where this conversation was going.

"We have this amazing new teacher, Miss Stevens, she showed us a movie at school, about people with diabetes," said Gemma enthusiastically "they got better eating raw food, it was really funny and…"

Rupert cut in rudely. "That is rubbish, I can't believe the crap they teach you." He was clearly angry and excused himself from the table.

"Now look what you've done," Gemma's mum glared at her as she spoke, as if her daughter was to blame for even trying to discuss medicine.

"But we did see a movie mum, it showed a bunch of diabetics, and they really did get better by simply changing their diets."

"Well I'm sure they did darling, but please don't upset your father ok."

20

A nice day off?

Dane Capper steered his bike along Franklin Road, taking his standard route to Jay's house for the after school surf. 'It has been a great day so far he' thought as he turned left into Beach Street. He noticed quite a few cars in the carpark and then he spotted Jay on the veranda checking the waves. He let himself in and went straight upstairs as usual.

"How'd you go mate?" he asked Jay, as he walked onto the veranda, referring to Jay's filming session.

"We got some ok footage, Paul was happy, he's already editing it. Waves are still ok now." Jay turned an accusing eye onto his mate, "what did you do today?"

"I actually went to the swimming carnival," Dane said sheepishly. "First time since Year 8." Although he would deny it under a penalty of death, he had hoped it would be an opportunity to bump into Miss Stevens.

"Let me see," Jay put his hands to his forehead like a mystic fortune teller. "I see a very hot teacher." He paused as if taking in his vision. "Don't tell me you missed good waves so you could see Miss Stevens?"

Dane felt as if Jay had read his mind and was now trying to read his face. "Of course not," he said unconvincingly.

"You have lost it mate, I knew it." Jay was exasperated...and then his curiosity got the better of him. "Well did you see her?"

"Yep, I did see her, she even told me I was one of her favourite students," Dane was clearly pleased with himself. "Miss told me she has just moved to Avondale and she loves it mate. Especially with students like me." Dane gave Jay a wink.

"Forget about that romantic crap Dane, was she in a bikini?" Jay got right to the point.

"No mate, no bikini, but she was just as…" Dane stopped to think and then continued. "You know what Jay, Miss Stevens is nothing less than the perfect woman."

"Don't forget, I saw her first," said Jay.

"Yeah but *then* she saw *me*, sorry mate." Dane pretended to be sad for Jay, he was always joking but the reality was he wouldn't want to be competing against Jay for any girl, even a teacher.

"Hey let's hit the waves Jay," as he spoke, Dane's phone lit up, it was Hobbsy so he quickly took the call.

"Hi Dane um, have you been on Facebook lately?" Barry asked mysteriously.

"Not lately Bazza," Dane hated Facebook. "Why what's up?"

Well the thing is your rap song is on the net, I filmed it on me phone, did a damn good job too, and I just thought the world had to see it. I hope that's ok?" asked Barry.

"You put our song on the net?" asked Dane. "You filmed it," he was obviously annoyed.

"The world deserved to see it," said Barry, who was always good with words. "People love it, they love you, I even said it the other day, you and Jay came off like rock stars. You would have been discovered sooner or later."

Hobbsy clearly thought he'd done the boys a favour. "Who doesn't want to be a rock star Dane?" he asked somewhat puzzled by his attitude. "If the cap fits, wear it," said Hobbsy, who was always coming up with those kinds of sayings.

"Yeah, I guess you are right," said Dane. He looked over at Jay who was giggling at whatever was on his IPhone. "How many hits?" asked Dane.

"It's already had thousands of likes and lots of shares. Check the clip, you guys look cool and you are helping the planet. I'll text you and Jay the link. Oh and Dane, you better watch yourselves," Barry cautioned, "you might get mobbed by fans."

Dane suddenly felt a bit concerned about Jay's sponsors and then, he noticed Jay snickering.

"Hey Jay, what's so funny?" Jay had been scrolling through his Facebook messages. I've had three messages from 'The Mermaid,' check it out." He gestured and Dane saw an intriguing and attractive girl who did indeed appear to be dressed as a mermaid in her photo.

"The Mermaid tells me she just loves *Planet Earth it's a Garden of Eden* and she loves me for standing up for our Planet."

"Did I miss something?" he looked at Dane for an explanation.

"Our clip's on the net mate, the rap song has already thousands of likes, I hope that's ok with your sponsors mate, I only just found out," Dane was still blown away himself.

"Hobbsy?"

Dane nodded at Jay to indicate that he had guessed right.

"Righto," Jay said, "let's watch it." He followed the link and started the clip on his IPhone. Hobbsy had done a great job, the filming was steady and the sound was pretty good. Jay and Dane were blown away by the clip, they sounded good and it was pretty funny. They looked pretty cool and it was a great message. The boys were actually pretty stoked about it.

Jay placed his IPhone carefully on the table. "Later Mermaid," he said and then playfully started wrestling Dane and giving him some quick punches in the ribs.

"You went to the Swimming Carnival, I still can't believe it."

21

General Studies: ivy talks on animal cruelty

Ivy Watkins took a deep breath as she prepared to start her presentation. Not at all embarrassed, she gave the class a beautiful smile, enchanting most of the boys, especially Mike Waters who had loved Ivy since second class. She was well liked and respected although some of the girls called her an emo, because she was sensitive, and also because of her raven hair and creamy white skin.

According to Ivy, one very good way to make the world a better place would be to stop whaling and halt all cruelty to animals. Ivy's message was clear. Harming animals is cruel and it harms us because as Albert said the other day, 'we are all part of the web of life.'

Despite her usually quiet personality, Ivy spoke confidently to her classmates. She was obviously speaking from the heart.

Ivy then showed a clip from *The Cove,* an award winning documentary about the slaughter of dolphins in Japan. It features Ric O'Barry, the man who trained the dolphins in the successful TV show called Flipper which was a big hit in the 1970's. Ric now spends his life trying to get all dolphins released from captivity.

The Cove starred popular young actress Hayden Paniterre and won the Oscar Award for Best Documentary in 2009. Paniterre and others were forcibly removed as they tried to expose the Cove, a place where around 2,300 dolphins and small whales are butchered every year. The filmmakers then went back and used state of the art spying techniques to film the Cove and obtain proof of the slaughter. A barbaric killing of beautiful creatures.

THE COVE

"How can Japanese people let this happen?" asked Gemma Healey.

"They kill heaps of whales as well," said Jacob Vaughan. "Like, what's their problem?"

Whilst no creature should suffer, Ivy pointed out that whales and dolphins have a unique impact on the Earth's energy field through the special nature of the sounds they make.

"They are beautiful intelligent wonderful creatures," she said sadly.

"According to the Cove, the dolphin meat is full of mercury, which is very poisonous. Independent random tests found the dolphin meat to contain 3 to 3500 times the levels deemed safe by the Japanese Government. How could dolphins be slaughtered and their contaminated meat sold to school lunch programs and grocery stores?

How can people do this for money?" despair was evident in Ivy's voice.

'These people are butchering dolphins *and* poisoning their children,' thought Crystal. She had to take a few deep breaths as the power of the movie overcame her. Glancing around the class she saw that everyone was incredibly moved by the footage. A couple of the girls were crying and some of the guys were really angry.

Sensing the need for something positive Ivy showed more of the story, this time about two brave Japanese men who fought the system and eventually stopped the dolphin meat, high in mercury, being served in Japanese schools. The class had a really good discussion about this.

"It shows how important it is to make a stand," said Barry Hobbs, "I mean, these guys stood up and stopped the kids from getting poisoned. How brave is that?"

"That's right," said Crystal. "What these people did was incredible, the movie makers, the two Japanese men, and also the way they have encouraged people from all over the world to write letters about the slaughter."

"What about the Japanese people?" asked Crystal, knowing this would fuel more debate. Some students thought that we should hassle Japanese people for *allowing* this to happen? In fact, Jay had actually seen two Japanese surfers get punched because of the whaling.

"That's crazy," said Ivy. "Most Japanese people interviewed in The Cove simply didn't know about the dolphin slaughter. I bet it's the same with the whaling, they probably don't know about that either. Maybe if they did know, they would be horrified just like us, maybe they would even try to stop it?"

"You know, it really shows how important the media is," said Dane. "Something this terrible should be world news. We only hear about the whaling when people like Greenpeace ram into the whaling boats. We need some sort of people's media, media that is actually true. It's just mental, we need to know about these real things, instead of the crap they feed us and call news."

Crystal appreciated the maturity and depth of the students' comments.

"Dane is raising some very good points, what we think we know is really what the media tells us. There is now a wave of new movies trying to get the truth out there.

Has anyone seen the new movie called Thrive?" asked Crystal, explaining that, "Thrive was made by Foster Gamble (his ancestor co-founded Procter & Gamble, one of the world's biggest companies, so he grew up as part of the wealthy elite)."

She continued, "Even though Foster Gamble was safe and secure, he wanted to try to work out why there is so much suffering in the world. After decades of research, he spent eight years making the movie, which concludes that much of the suffering is because everything is deliberately controlled by a few people who keep us powerless and distracted. The movie puts its arguments forward logically and with expert support. It's definitely worth checking out.

Ok, we need to wind down for lunch. That was an amazing presentation, thank you so much Ivy."

Ivy handed her a hard copy of her notes and then Crystal added. "I hope you all have a Happy Valentine's Day, I'll see you on Thursday. Dane is presenting...Dane?" she looked at him for clarification.

"Yeah Miss, too easy, Thursday, this stuff about needing true information is exactly what I'll be talking about," said Dane thinking quickly, as he hadn't actually worked out what he would talk about. Later as they were walking out to lunch, Jay reminded the boys how pleased he was to have gone first.

"I'm so glad I'm already done," he said smugly.

"Hey Jay," said Hobbsy, "maybe you can do a rap song for Dane?"

"Ah...nup," said Jay, pretending to give the matter some thought.

"I'll be off school on Thursday, it's the Natural Rhythm Pro," he said. This was actually a massive opportunity for Jay as a major pro surfing event was being held at his home beach next weekend, and the qualifying rounds were on Thursday and Friday.

22

Craig and Tina at lunch

Craig and Tina both bought lunch from home so they didn't need to bother with the canteen. They sat in the exact same spot as they had for the past two weeks and chatted away about Ivy's presentation.

"I really agree with Dane you know," said Craig. "We all assume that the media tells us truth and that they tell us everything important but what about the things they don't tell us."

They talked about different ways to incorporate this into a movie, and about how cool Miss Stevens is.

"It's the most interesting subject by far," said Tina. "She even wished us all a Happy Valentine's Day, how cool is that!"

Tina's words reminded Craig of what he had planned. He had agonized about today because he didn't want to come on too strong but equally, he didn't want to disappoint Tina.

Vanessa had been at him to do something. "At least give her a card bro, girls love that stuff," she told him.

"But you said not to look too eager." Craig had been puzzled but Vanessa assured him Valentine's Day was different.

Craig reached for the envelope. "That reminds me," he said trying to act cool, even though his heart had probably never beaten faster than it was now, "Happy Valentine's Day Tina."

Craig had read that we communicate with our body

language just as much as we do with our words. He knew he had made the right choice microseconds after giving Tina the card. Her eyes showed her appreciation first and then her lovely smile confirmed it. Just for this once he was pleased that Vanessa was his sister.

Tina opened Craig's card:

> *"Dear Tina*
> *I'm glad I came to this new school*
> *Meeting you was super cool*
>
> *I'm not real good at this sort of thing*
> *But time with you makes me want to sing*
>
> *And every time I see your face*
> *My world becomes a better place.*
>
> *HAPPY VALENTINES DAY FROM YOUR NOT SO SECRET ADMIRER.*
>
> *CRAIG XX"*

Tina could not help herself, she started to cry but then when Craig said, "Wow, that bad huh?" Tina started to laugh as well. She was a mess.

"It's lovely Craig, thank you, I didn't, well, Valentine's Day is not something we really talked about in our house this year," Tina finished talking and then started to cry again.

Craig realized it was the first Valentine's Day since Tina's mum had died. He put his hand on Tina's shoulder.

"It's OK Tina, I understand," he said tenderly. Tina burst out laughing,

"I'm such an idiot," she said, her wonderful infectious laugh causing Craig to laugh as well.

They chatted happily until the bell went reminding them that they were at school and had to go to their next class. As it so happened, the school had its first big assembly of the year after lunch, so Craig and Tina filed into the School Auditorium with all the other students and teachers.

23

School Assembly

Craig Sceats was amazed at the size of the auditorium. He whispered to Tina "Avondale has lots more kids than our last two schools put together." He sat and took it all in, ever grateful to be sitting with his lovely new friend.

Mr. Rawles, the unpopular Deputy Principal made a speech welcoming the new Year 7 kids, and congratulating the new Year 12's on finally having the run of the playground. After finishing what he wanted to say, Mr. Rawles called on the Sports Master Ken Anderson to present some outstanding sporting achievement awards. It was Tina's turn to whisper to Craig.

"Ando is a real legend; he's so great at motivating the kids."

Ando called out three names and those kids made their way up on stage. Jay Williams stood side by side with Albert Rose, as Ando presented an award to Caitlin Jones of Year 9 for being a runner up in the Australian Junior Titles of tennis. Ando spoke about Caitlin's achievements and then looked up at the audience.

"How good is that? Congratulations Caitlin."

Next up was Albert. Albert had been selected as halfback in the NSW schoolboys side (pretty good for a Year 10 student at that time). It was clear in his voice, Ken Anderson thought the world of Albert. He was confident that Albert would lead the school team to another successful year, and was already tipping Albert to have a first grade career.

"Last but certainly not least, Jay Williams," said Mr Anderson, to rousing cheers from the audience. Jay was onstage courtesy of his win at last year's World Schoolboy Titles in California.

"Jay is our very own world champion. He won every heat he surfed in a wide range of conditions and even had girls chasing him after his heats," said his awed Sportsmaster.

Had Craig been watching his sister, he would have recognized the way she looked at Jay.

"Mmm," she said to her friends Rosie and Susie, "no wonder those American girls were chasing him." Vanessa already had three anonymous Valentine's Day cards from secret admirers. She and Rosie and Suzie guessed that they were guys in her classes, which was nice, but as Craig well knew, Vanessa would typically go after someone older and way cooler. It was more of a challenge.

Her previous school was in Albury, where awards for skateboarding or skiing were far more common than for surfing. Vanessa had gone round with Todd Brennan, the best skateboarder in the school. He was a really cool guy and he had a tattoo. Todd was in Year 11, so he was two years older as well.

"You just like the limelight of being with the best skater in the school," Craig had admonished her at the time, but he had to admit, Vanessa did seem cut up about leaving Todd. That seemed like a long time ago, it was already the third week of term, Craig would have expected Vanessa to have at least one target by now.

24

Maths Class

Craig sat with Tina towards the back of their maths room. The class was doing algebra that nobody seemed to understand. Without exception, the kids had their heads down, each hoping, praying even, that Mr Southwell would not ask them a question. He seemed on edge, nervously pacing back and forward in front of the class.

A note was being passed around and an increasing number of students began to snicker. Mr Southwell was now in front of Jacob, scrutinizing his work while everyone was trying not to burst out laughing.

"Mr Vaughan," he boomed, "your work is all over the place like a mad women's breakfast." Jacob probably had no idea what that even meant. He was probably hoping Mr Southwell would turn his attention elsewhere, when the gods smiled upon him by making that happen.

Trained from many years of teaching, Mr Southwell's eagle eyes spotted Debbie Jones just as she was handing a note to Naomi Tate. His attention was diverted, much to Jacob's relief.

"Ms Jones, I assume you are handing Ms Tate the answer to this problem," he said as Deb's life started to flash before her eyes. "Ms Tate and Jones, please come forward." Both girls sat frozen with fear. He demanded that they bring him the note.

As the class watched on in horror, Naomi bravely walked towards Mr Southwell.

"What's so funny?" he asked a few kids in the back corner who were smirking and finding it increasingly difficult not to laugh. Nobody answered. Everyone was spellbound as he ordered Naomi to read the note. Her lips quivered and her voice trembled with fear as she read:

'Sir's fly is undone.'

An expression of horror crossed his brow as he looked down and noticed the familiar pattern of his tartan undershorts. He then seemed to realize that the whole class was watching. The class could no longer restrain themselves and they all just roared with laughter.

Mr Southwell turned the colour of freshly cut beetroot and left the room, presumably to do his pants back up. Naomi was hailed as a hero as was Barry Hobbs, who had written the note. The class eventually calmed down. They knew it would be wise to be working hard when and if Mr Southwell did come back.

25

Old Maids on Valentine's Night

That night Crystal reflected on Ivy's presentation, it was excellent as was her written submission. The thing that made Crystal happiest of all was the overall enthusiasm of the kids. She had been warned by some of the other teachers that just getting the kids to choose a topic in General Studies would be like pulling teeth. The reality was a pleasant surprise for Crystal who had no idea about the coming storm.

"Look at us," Beth joked. "Here having dinner together at home on Valentine's Day, just like a pair of old maids."

Crystal laughed at this, "I'm too busy to even think about men, and besides, you do enough of that for both of us Bethany."

Beth was a yoga teacher and personal trainer. She had lots of guys try to ask her out, but she was pretty choosy and seemed to just enjoy the thrill of the chase. At any time, there were always a couple of prospects, such as *new guy from yoga* or *hot waiter at the organic cafe*. Crystal regularly debated their merits with Beth, often without meeting or seeing them.

From what Crystal could see Beth simply enjoyed flirting with guys. So far, the only guy Crystal had even mentioned to Beth was the 'hot guy from the beach,' on the morning of her first day of teaching. She had gushed to Beth about the surfer and would now die of embarrassment if Beth ever found out that he was one of her students. She changed the subject whenever Beth asked about him. 'What a shame,' thought Crystal, Jay really is hot.

Beth had hired *'Pretty Woman,'* a great romantic movie for the two old maids to watch together. It's one of Crystal's favourite movies and she enjoyed it just as much as every other time she had seen it.

Happy Valentine's Day.

26

Can we really thrive?

That night, Dane Capper watched Thrive with his eldest brother Simon. Simon still lived fulltime at the stately manor, the name someone had given to Capper's parents' original sandstone mansion, based on Batman's famous Stately Wayne Manor. The name had stuck and now everyone used it.

Since his dad had retired, Dane's parents were always away, catching up on their traveling, which was something they had always wanted to do. Most nights, it was just Simon and Dane staying at the stately manor. Technically, his older sister Jasmine still lived there, however, she was a full time university student and most nights through the week, Jasmine stayed with friends who lived near the university.

As you might expect of someone still living at his parents and watching Thrive with his younger brother on Valentine's Day, Simon Capper was very much still a bachelor. He worked with the National Parks and Wildlife Department, a great job because he was passionate about nature, but not an ideal job to meet women.

Dane had a whole 'wing' of the house to himself. Apparently, it used to be the 'servants quarters' when the house was originally built in the 1850's. His mates loved to come around so they could play their music as loud as they wanted.

As Foster Gamble's story of our controlled society unfolded before them, even Simon was getting angry. They learned about devices which could produce energy without electricity or oil. Endless power. No pollution.

THRIVE

The Producers included segments on numerous inventors who had actual working inventions, but the story was always the same, once they had announced and promised their *free energy*, they had been harassed and forced to stop their work. Laboratories were burned down and inventions were confiscated by the American Government, all in the *interests of National Security*.

"How could this happen? It defies all reason and logic," said Dane. "How could Governments simply confiscate free energy devices? It makes no sense, these are devices that could save our world and feed all the starving people.

Ok, the confiscation of devices is history but why not get the plans back now," suggested Dane. "Just start using them now for the future. I mean, are they saying it's possible to totally give free energy to the world and people just don't do it?"

"You are spot on brother, people just don't do it," said Simon. "The people who run things are not going to make changes, and nobody tries to force them to."

"Those bastards might run the system," said Dane, "but without the masses they exploit, there would be no system". Dane was right, he knew it, and so did Simon. "If you think about it, the many should be able to have control because of their numbers," said Dane. "After all," he continued, "they are the *workforce* and the *consumers* that the whole system runs on. Without their active participation, there is no system."

"Yes, but how will they ever know to get together if the media does not want them to?" said Simon, shaking his head sadly.

"Because we'll spread the word," said Dane sounding wise beyond his years.

FREE ENERGY

"We'll tell the *many* how to beat the *few*," Dane added triumphantly.

Dane went over to his part of the house and went online. His searching confirmed what Thrive had said. There were free energy devices (also called new energy devices), which literally borrow energy from space. No Explosion. No Pollution. There was much debate about it and of course, people are always sceptical about anything new but the point was, *why as a society do we not give free energy the resources and support that we should?*

Dane found *A Universal Appeal for Support for New Energy Science and Technology,* sent to the world by Dr. Eugene F. Mallove, a passionate scientist with excellent qualifications including a Master of Science from MIT and a Doctor of Science from Harvard.

This inspirational and comprehensive ten page document discussed our *free energy* potential with hope, optimism and courage. Dane's inspiration soon turned to horror when he read that this great man, who worked so hard for free energy causes, was brutally murdered not long after writing his Universal Appeal.

'Bloody hell,' thought Dane, that is super heavy. Dane actually found a website compiled by one journalist, which listed many suspicious deaths of new energy inventors and supporters. 'These big guys don't muck around,' thought Dane.

UNIVERSAL APPEAL TO SUPPORT FREE ENERGY

He really had this thing in his head about the *many* taking back control from the *few*. He was sure they would unite given half a chance. It's just about how you communicate with everyone. The television networks and newspaper moguls are not thinking about how to inform the *many*, they represent the *few*. Like Simon said, they make the rules the way they want them.

I wish there was a simple way to show the people their true power. It was time to fight back. Dane was totally consumed by his research, there was so much information. He finally logged off just before midnight, pretty late for a school night. It took him a little while to wind down then he drifted off into a very deep sleep.

Dane was dreaming when his alarm went off. In his dream, he had seen waves and waves of teenagers demanding truth from their parents, their Government and their society. They were all dressed in white and were chanting

> *"the Younger Generation have to Unite*
> *because the Older Generation just can't get it right".*

They were demanding answers about the fluoride in the water. The dream had shown him the power of teenagers as a united force. Dane knew what he had to do.

27

Dane prepares

Dane spent the next two afternoons and evenings researching for his presentation. By Wednesday he knew what he wanted to say, and sat at the computer collating it into a PowerPoint. Dane was certain that people had a duty to help the world by *waking up*, by taking responsibility for their own consciousness, not being zombies who believe everything the media tells them.

People need to demand changes on behalf of their planet. The problem is that people are not even suspicious because they think that everything is perfect already. Their only source of information in most cases is television, newspapers and the internet. This is not reality, it's programming.

The fluoride situation was a perfect one to use in his presentation because it was so corrupt, so newsworthy, and so relevant to why we are a sick society and yet, so ignored. It was all there in black and white and yet there was nothing but a deafening silence.

Just like new energy, and the whaling, it's always people doing bad things because they get money, or save money. Money is like our god, it seems to rule everything. We are letting them get away with murder thought Dane. *'Well we **were** letting them, but not anymore.'*

Dane lay in bed running through his presentation in his head. He was excited about tomorrow and couldn't wait to impress Miss Stevens. He dozed off to sleep, unaware that at that very moment, a movement known as *Occupy* and representing all of the things he thought about, was quietly gathering momentum around the world.

THE OCCUPY MOVEMENT

28

General Studies : Dane has his say

Dane Capper's presentation was entitled *It's time to wake up*. He had a witty opening slide which satirised the movie 'The Sixth Sense', showing a child cowering under her blankets with the caption *I See Dumb People*. Everyone laughed right off the bat. It was a nice start.

Dane's voice was clear and powerful, "people accept everything they are told. They believe the media is gospel truth, but really, it's a carefully controlled message of what *they* want you to hear."

"Amen to that," said Jacob Vaughan.

"We are being brainwashed and distracted by a system that runs on money," said Dane. "That's how every decision gets made."

He showed a trailer for the movie *Who Killed the Electric Car,* a movie about the invention and suppression of an electric car. The cars worked really well and people were lining up to buy them but the car company, obviously under pressure from someone, still went ahead and crushed them all for scrap metal.

"So what happens when the car company's decision can potentially affect the whole planet?" said Dane.

"That's a really good point Dane," said Crystal, "there is a conflict of interest between profits and the planet."

Dane explained the shady history of fluoridation, which is a classic example of this conflict.

"They have now discovered old memos from companies producing toxic waste. They were copping flack for dumping it in rivers and they couldn't dump it in the ocean. They convinced the world to let them put it in their water.

"Now that must have been one hell of a sales pitch," said Hobbsy, causing Crystal and the students to laugh.

WHO KILLED THE ELECTRIC CAR

He continued in a comedic voice, "What's that? You want to put toxic waste in our water? Oh yeah, sure, as long as you say it's good for our teeth, we don't care what it does to the rest of our bodies," Hobbsy rolled his eyes sarcastically. They all laughed again.

Once everyone gained their composure, Dane continued,

In Australia, babies that aren't breastfed may drink formula mixed in fluoridated water without any warning. This is a big risk at a crucial time of brain development and growth as fluoride has been shown to cross the blood brain barrier. Even the American Dental Association seems to discourage mothers from feeding babies with fluoridated water. It makes you wonder why this risk is never even mentioned in Australia?"

Dane talked about a great new documentary called *Firewater: Australia's Industrial Flouride Disgrace*. He showed a clip of Dr Andrew Harms, former president of the Australian Dental Association South Australian Branch, who admits that he was wrong to ever endorse fluoridation, and in particular, said:

"I didn't realise that we were not using natural fluoride,

> *but we were using a common industrial waste, coming*
> *from the superphosphate industry and also industrial waste*
> *from China, the origins of which we do not know. It is not*
> *pharmaceutical grade, its industrial grade".*

What are the dentists other than Dr Harms thinking? Well, he says in the movie that they don't want to say anything to upset their sponsors.

To lighten the mood, Dane clicked on a humorous slide showing a hideous Zombie with beautiful teeth saying *Poison your brain to get good teeth*

The class laughed again and so did Crystal. "The thing is," Dane revealed "many experts say it's not even good for your teeth anyway."

Dane grew serious as he told them how more than 50 years ago, a man named Edward Bernays wrote a book about 'Controlling the Public.' He said that it was necessary for the *intelligent few* to control the *many*.

"At one point, the tobacco companies hired him to increase their sales and he deliberately hired doctors to tell people that smoking was healthy. You can easily find the old ads online" said Dane as he clicked on an ad showing a group of doctors recommending Camel cigarettes as a healthy choice.

"Think how many people were told smoking was safe and then died of cancer."

"Bernays is the guy they hired to sell fluoride," said Dane to Miss Stevens and the class, continuing dramatically, "and we *believed him* when he said it's good for us."

"Are we mental?" said Hobbsy in a sarcastic voice.

"Good question," said Dane "I think we are."

Dane started a clip of Dr Paul Connett, a renowned specialist in Toxicology (poisons), whose wife nagged him for years to look at the fluoride situation. 'You are a poisons specialist for goodness sake,' she told the good doctor, who kept refusing, he was too busy and in his words:

'Up to that point, I thought the people opposed to fluoridation were a bunch of wackos.'

"This shows how powerful their brainwashing is. It was only his wife's persistence that could even get this highly qualified man to look at fluoridation and in his own words, when he did, he was *shocked and embarrassed.*

CONTROLLING THE MASSES WITH PROPOGANDA

He discovered little, if any, benefit for teeth, explaining how studies suggesting this were very misleading by modern testing standards. Sodium fluoride actually causes big problems for our brains and bones and our pineal and thyroid glands.

The mention of the *pineal gland* caused Tina to raise her hand. "My mum was a doctor and she told me how important the pineal gland is to our consciousness," said Tina.

"That is exactly right Tina," said Dane, then he put on a funny voice trying to make light of a serious situation.

"They're dumbing us down so we learn to drink beer and watch TV."

Everyone was laughing except Crystal, who was thinking about what Tina's mum had said. 'Her mum must be quite the new age doctor.'

The next thing Dane spoke about was hypnosis.

DR PAUL CONNETT

"Our beliefs define us and yet we get them fed to us. You all know about hypnosis right, the person who is hypnotized acts in a funny way because of what they are told to believe. People think they are dogs and cats and stuff. One guy was hypnotized to not see his mate, and later when his mate smoked a cigar as part of the performance, he only saw a lit cigar with nobody smoking it.

"It's that powerful," said Dane.

"Hey I saw that," said Hobbsy, giving Dane support and encouragement. "I also saw the guy who was told by the hypnotist that he couldn't pick up a glass of water. It was so funny, he might as well have been trying to lift a swimming pool." The whole class laughed and then Dane became serious.

"Just think of how our powerful belief systems are continually programmed by vested interests. I reckon our whole society is hypnotized. Hypnotized by the power of the media," he said sadly.

"Now I can really see why the elders tell *the story* generation to generation by word of mouth," said Albert, "word of mouth is the only way to preserve the truth."

"That is true wisdom brother," said Dane. "We need truth and we need it now. Teenagers need to be awake and feel for ourselves what our true beliefs are."

Again, the class burst into loud applause and Dane Capper gave a little bow.

29

Friday afternoon

Friday afternoon signalled the end of the third week of school. Dane rode his bike straight to Jay's to see how he went in the surfing competition. Peddling strongly, he was quietly confident that Jay had made it through to the weekend's main event. He was excited about that and the gathering he was going to that night.

Dane walked straight up the steps to find Jay sitting with his coach Darren watching a replay of his heats.

"Hey hey hey, Dane, this bloke will be surfing again tomorrow against the big boys." Darren's voice boomed across the room, he was clearly one proud coach.

"Whew!" Dane's face lit up. "I knew you'd make it Jay. You'll be Natural Rhythm Pro Champ by this time Sunday I reckon." He gave his best mate a high five.

"Let's take it one heat at a time," said Darren sensibly.

Jay showed Dane the footage of his heats so far, including a ten point ride for two crazy aerial manoeuvres in Round Three *(aerial manoeuvres meaning that the surfer actually flies through the air attached to the surfboard, lands and keeps on going)*.

"You got a ten? Wow. Stick the knife in at your home beach bro, nice one." Dane was totally stoked for his mate.

"Yeah," said Jay modestly, "and I can't make tonight's party aye.

Darren's having dinner here, I think he wants to make sure I crash early. Maybe I can win some good coin?"

"I'll have fun for you mate," said Dane who, wanting to inspire Jay, added, "there'll be another party next week mate, but this contest won't be on again for another year, if ever, so make the most of it. We'll celebrate on Sunday Night." Dane gave Jay a wink, he knew he had an ok chance on his home beach provided nerves did not get the better of him.

30

Who is that girl?

Anne and Greg Barnes had decided to have another one of their famous gatherings. "It's not a party," said Greg.

"Just a few friends," said Anne, giggling at her brother. Greg was in Year 12 and Anne Year 10. Their parents had a weekend away every month, visiting their new granddaughter in Canberra.

"How convenient of sis to move down there," said Anne gratefully.

Greg played in a muck around band with his mates. They didn't really have a name so as a joke, they called themselves 'no name,' and it stuck. Dane Capper played lead guitar, Jacob Vaughan played base, and Lance Halloran played drums. Lance was known affectionately as 'the Animal,' after the wild Muppets character. 'No name' always played at Greg and Anne's gatherings.

People began to arrive at the Barnes' place at around seven. As always, Greg and Anne invited particular people from Year 10 and 12, warning everyone not to pass on any general invitations. Why spoil a good thing. After so much practice, the gatherings were organised like a well-oiled machine.

Anne was in the same English class as Rosie and Suzie and their lovely new friend Vanessa Sceats, so those three girls were all invited. A few of Greg's male and female friends from year 12 also came over, plus a few mates and girls who were friends of the band.

The band was getting ready as the crowd gathered. No name

had a limited number of songs, and so, tended to play them all again in each of their three or four sets. As you would expect, they played simple and catchy songs like Deep Purple's 'Smoke on the Water' and the White Stripes' 'Seven Nation Army'. That was Jacob's favourite, because the prominent base riff made him feel like a rock star.

They also covered some Beatles and Rolling Stones and best of all for Capper, a Dire Straits song with a really good lead guitar solo. Greg's voice sounded ok and so did Dane's when he chose to also sing along. Everyone was having a good time.

Vanessa and her pals danced to every song in the first set. The boys had played at Greg's lots of times and knew Anne and her friends. They didn't usually pay them much attention, but that was definitely not the case tonight.

The new girl was performing for the band just as they were performing for her. She looked sexy in a grunge ensemble of very short shorts, black gym boots and a Led Zeppelin print singlet top she borrowed from her brother Craig.

Her friends were trying to keep up with her, but Vanessa seemed to be ignoring everyone and staying in her own little bubble. She had Dane and the boys captivated as they finished another song and announced a short break.

Dane was following the others over to their drink cooler when Vanessa caught his eye. She smiled and told him, "that was so much fun."

"Cheers," replied Dane modestly. "Hey nice top, I dig Led Zeppelin," he added.

"Thanks," said Vanessa smiling at Dane. "I dig... *Teenager's for Truth*," she said tentatively, after taking a moment to read his shirt.

"I'm gonna get a drink, you want one?" he asked Vanessa.

"Yeah sure," she said as her friends looked on in awe of her confidence. She followed Dane over to the cooler and he reached in and grabbed two icy cold drinks.

"You guys rock." Vanessa had clearly enjoyed the band.

"Well we're going to do an original song next. It's a bit of a protest song and the thing is," said Dane sincerely, "we are trying to get other teenagers to join our cause."

"I'll join," she replied enthusiastically. "Well, that is, provided your song is not too bad. I love a good protest." Vanessa's smile was mischievous.

"Thanks for the drink, I'm just going to catch up with my friends for a minute. Excuse me."

She breezed past confidently leaving Dane to catch up with his band mates, who were a little jealous he'd spoken to Vanessa before them.

"Dude, that chick is so smoking," said Jacob. "Well, she's my sister's friend," said Greg Barnes, as if that gave him some sort of claim over Vanessa. "That means zilch Barnesy and you know it bro," said Dane.

The boys hassled each other good naturedly while they finished their drinks. Dane got things organized for the protest song which was of course his rap song. He insisted the whole band put on the *'Teenagers for Truth'* t-shirts he had made with his sister's silk screen press. He also put on his favourite cap, backwards of course.

"OK. This one's a protest song," said Dane, as Vanessa and the other girls walked over towards the band.

"I got a question for you," said Dane trying to sound like Jim Morrison (the rebellious singer from the Doors, a famous band from the 70's).

"Just what are the oldies doing and just how totally screwed up is this planet?"

Dane's eyes were hazel. They sometimes appeared to be green in the daylight, but at this moment, they looked brown and filled with fire. His longish dark brown hair was soaked with sweat. He held the microphone in his right hand like a man possessed, and he raised his left hand into the air. He spoke his message as the crowd cheered.

"It's about time something was done," he told the crowd, "and we're gonna do it. Yeah. We are the younger generation and we're gonna do it.

YEAH !!"

Everyone cheered and the band launched into *Planet Earth it's a Garden of Eden*. To accompany the lyrics and backing tape, Dane had come up with a simple sequence of chords which he had run through briefly with the boys earlier in the night. Vanessa and the girls started singing along to the chorus:

"The Younger Generation has to Unite
because the Older Generation just can't get it right".

As the song wound down, Jacob, Greg and 'the Animal' did exactly as Dane had said, each repeating the last line of a different verse 3 times over. Lines like "What about our kids, that just ain't fair?" and, "If man could keep his bargain the planet would thrive!" repeated after each other, over and over, getting softer and softer. It was a brilliant idea, to finish the song, it sounded professional.

As the song stopped, Dane began freestyle rapping to the crowd. He was fired up and making add libbed verses about all sorts of things, including pollution, parents and teachers. Then he turned his mic to his Local Member of Parliament.

"Ok listen up. Our local member Doug Toovey is coming to the beach on Sunday for the presentation of the Natural Rhythm Pro. Let's get everyone we know and go down and ask him what he's doing to help the planet. I wanna ask him about fluoride and show him a DVD. You know what?" yelled Dane.

"We're gonna tell Mr Doug Toovey
That we have a question or three;
We're gonna ask him right to his face
What's going on with the Toxic Waste?
YEAH !!
We hope to see you there," said Dane.

Dane saluted the crowd and then led 'no name' in a song they had practiced but never played to an audience. A rousing version of Silver Chair's 'Wait till Tomorrow'. Dane and Greg nailed the vocals, it was fantastic.

When the second set finished, Vanessa grabbed a bottle of water and took a big sip as Dane once again walked towards her.

"That was unreal," she said, "oh, and by the way, I'm Vanessa."

Her eyes sparkled invitingly and she continued to hold Dane's hand after they shook.

"I'm Dane," he said feeling like putty in her fingers. They were both drenched in sweat.

Vanessa had been to Anne's before and she knew the layout of the house.

"Follow me," she whispered in Dane's ear.

Still holding his hand, Vanessa led him around to the other side of the house to the Barnes' swimming pool.

'Who are you,' thought Dane as he watched her take off her boots then her shorts and then her singlet. She dived into the pool in her underwear. Capper needed no further encouragement. He stripped down to his Calvin Kleins and dived in after her.

The water was beautiful and Vanessa swam right up to Dane. "What a magic night," she whispered and then kissed him gently on the lips. Dane responded enthusiastically.

They were kissing in waist deep water when they were suddenly interrupted by Anne and Rosie.

"Oops," giggled Anne. Vanessa and Dane stopped and looked at the girls.

Vanessa was holding her arms in front of her chest, covering her bra. She was starting to shiver.

"Let's get back to the party," she said, clearly annoyed at the interruption. Anne was back in a flash with two towels and Vanessa and Dane dried off. He couldn't help staring at her.

"So where did you come from?" he asked sounding slightly bewildered. Each answer from Vanessa left him more intrigued. They took their own good time and chatted happily, leaving Anne and Rosie just standing there waiting. They walked back in to the party and everyone stared at Vanessa and Dane, soaking wet and smiling like Cheshire cats.

31

Jay against the big boys

Dane Capper woke up early, ate a quick breakfast and then headed down to Jay's. The Natural Rhythm Pro was on in clean four foot waves right in front of Jay's parents' house. He stood his bike against Jay's garage wall and headed straight over to the beach.

He saw Jay and Darren, obviously trying to get a read on the conditions before Jay's heat. Jay was in Heat Seven. Because he was not on the World Professional Surfing Tour, Jay was the lowest seed in the event. Under the seeding rules, Jay would automatically face the highest seed, World Champion Robert Slade.

This was obviously a tough draw for Jay but the word on the street was that the champ had an ankle injury. Slade hadn't been warming up at *Avo*, as most of the pros called it.

"Don't forget," said Darren adding as an afterthought, "Round One is non-elimination, you have nothing to lose Jay, have some fun mate." "Good Luck," said Dane feeling a little nervous for his mate, but then adding reassuringly,

"Jay, it's your bloody beach."

As soon as the heat started, Jay lucked into a great set wave. The other competitors were caught off guard sitting a bit too far in and missed the whole set.

'So, local knowledge really does pay off,' thought Dane as Jay went to town on his wave, a wave which held up longer than most that morning. A huge air reverse right off the take-off followed by two powerful top turns and then an 'alley oop,' in the shore break that Jay deftly landed before literally jumping off on the sand. Nice. The commentators loved it and so did the judges, awarding 9.5 out of 10. A bow to the crowd would not have been out of place but Jay was too modest for that.

Jay was able to back his 9.5 up with a 7, giving him 16.5, a strong win and the second highest heat total of the morning. He was straight through to Round 3, thus avoiding the deadly losers round.

The wave gods of Avondale had been kind to their current favourite son. Jay was stoked. He was almost mobbed after the heat and spent over ten minutes signing autographs.   Rob Slade had even come over to Jay and shaken his hand and wished him well for the rest of the event. Eventually Jay and Dane walked back to his house leaving Darren to stay and watch a few more heats.

Once they were alone Jay admitted to Dane, "I was actually super nervous, especially surfing against the world champion. Then I got that first wave and the nerves just disappeared."

"I told you bro, we'll be celebrating tomorrow night." Dane's belief in his best mate was unwavering. They ate and played pool as they would on any other day, seemingly a million miles from the circus across the road.

Dane also filled Jay in on last night's party, especially about Vanessa dragging him into the pool.

"You are a stud," said Jay. Dane laughed modestly. "It was a fun night mate, but it's obviously good you hung with Darren, a 9.5, what a way to start the day.....your first wave in the big time and now you're in Round 3. Whew."

Jay's Round Three heat was the last of the day. He had a great skipping warm up, put on his boardshorts and walked across the road to *his* beach. He checked in and collected his singlet.

Jay was against Dino Knox, a tour veteran who they thought might struggle to match Jay's new school moves.

"This guy's gonna hassle you heaps Jay, he knows you're the local boy, maybe you should paddle him all over the place," said Darren.

"I don't know," said Jay, "I reckon I'll just stay out of his way."

Jay did just that and scraped through the wave starved heat.

Dane was delighted, he knew Jay's own personal target to make it through to the final day and now he'd done it. Darren looked like he was going to cry.

The Network News even wanted to interview Jay; he was the man of the hour. That night, Jay featured on the Nightly News Report, ripping the waves and then shaking Dino's hand. Talk about being a sponsor's dream, *their* kid in *their* contest at *his* beach.

"I might crash early again bro," he told Dane. "It could be a big day tomorrow," he added with massive understatement.

"I'll see you in the morning Jay," said Dane, wondering how his buddy kept so calm.

32

Saturday Night at Dane's

Dane was on his bike, not far from his house when he heard his phone beep inside his backpack. He pulled over and reached for his phone.

"Hi Dane. What's Up. Last night was cool. Ring me Vanessa X".

"Nice," thought Dane breaking into a wide grin. He had never met a girl like Vanessa, she was a real livewire. He phoned her and discovered she was with her friends. As he and Vanessa chatted, Dane realised that he really wanted to see her tonight, even if that meant having to put up with her friends. Why not he thought? He was so excited about Jay's success that he had to do something.

"Hey, you guys can come over if you want, I'm home alone."

The girls agreed to come over and so Dane, thinking it best to have at least one brother in arms, rang Jacob, who was home, free and happy to lend a hand.

Dane had so many ideas to write down and sing, he could see how the world needed to change. He was a crusader for truth. His heart raced as he thought of Vanessa, a thing of beauty in a world gone mad. She could be his muse.

Jacob arrived first and they started playing a backing track, each had a mic, taking turns to say whatever came into their heads, freestyle. They were laughing heaps and coming up with some great lines. Rosie's mum dropped the girls off and told them to text her when they needed a lift home.

"If I don't hear, I'll be back at eleven," she said as Rosie closed the door.

The front door is a long walk from Dane's 'wing' of the house so he and Jacob had to race to open the main door for the girls.

"What is this house, a museum?" asked Vanessa. "I love the sandstone bricks, how old is it?"

"It was built in the 1850's," said Dane. "C'mon, let's go back over to my part of the house."

The girls "oohed and aahed," as they followed Dane and Jacob back to where the boys had been having their concert.

"This house is truly amazing," said Suzie with genuine admiration.

"Looks like you've started already," said Anne, obviously noticing the microphones and tape deck.

"Dane's picked up where he left off last night and I'm trying to help a bit as well," said Jacob with a shy smile. Anne seemed to be sizing Jacob up as he spoke. She had carried a torch for Dane all through Year 10 but now, with Vanessa around, that could be tough.

Jacob was pretty quiet but he was handsome under all that hair. He was also funny and had a nice smile. Anne smiled right at him, as if thinking, 'I'll go for Jacob instead.' He returned Anne's gaze and told her everyone had to have a go at rapping but the girls were of course all saying 'no way.'

As it turned out, they were very impressed by Jacob and Dane and after their initial nerves, the girls all had turns on the mic as well. It was hilarious. A natural performer, Vanessa was making everything rhyme without worrying about the randomness of her words. Just saying anything that came into her head, she had the crowd completely entertained.

'Hey Doug,' she teased, pointing an accusing finger at the imaginary politician

'What's going on with our water?'
Why did you give it to your daughter?
Now she's gonna get cancer.
She could have been a pole dancer.'

With that line, she started to dance around an imaginary pole, graceful, cat like and yet provocative. When Vanessa realised everyone was staring, she stopped, burst out laughing and threw the mic to Suzie for her turn.

Vanessa had passion, Dane could feel it. He knew she would be an excellent recruit for Teens for Truth. He had some questions about fluoride written down to ask Doug Toovey tomorrow, so while they were having a break, Dane grabbed his notes and discussed them with the group. He wanted to ask questions that everyone would agree were important.

Dane wrote a single page and Vanessa added some doodles of hearts and flowers. Jacob drew a skull and Vanessa drew a tap above it, so the message was *drink the water and suffer.*

"Thanks guys," said Dane looking closely at the tap and skull. "That makes a pretty cool emblem." It looked so good that Dane decided to run off copies in the morning and get Vanessa and the girls to hand them out.

"So how many copies should I do?" asked Dane, looking at Vanessa

"I can be pretty persuasive," she countered confidently. "I'd bring quite a few if I were you."

"Ok, it's a deal," said Dane. Vanessa looked at Dane and said

"I'd rather get them to sign up, or like join the cause or a mailing list or something. It's much more fun trying to get their signature, more of a challenge."

"Brilliant idea" said Dane.

"We can get people to sign a petition asking Doug Toovey to explain about the fluoride and we can give him the movie to watch as well."

They sat and talked and laughed until they heard Rosie's mum's car horn just before eleven. The girls all spoke at once for the next minute.

"Thanks for having us Dane, that was so much fun."

"Yeah so much fun."

"You boys have got talent."

"I wouldn't want to be Doug Toovey."

"See you at the beach."

Finally, they were out the door. Vanessa blew Dane a kiss and then closed the door behind her.

"What are you man, a Casanova or something?" said a clearly blown away Jacob.

"I'm totally not complaining." Dane felt chuffed, like the cat that got the cream. He'd had a fun night after watching Jay make the finals. He felt immense gratitude and was indeed 'totally not complaining.'

"Hey Jacob, are you staying here?

"Yeah mate," Jacob said and then he pulled the spare mattress from under Dane's bed and unrolled Dane's sleeping bag, a routine he had been through many times. The boys talked and laughed about their day, their rapping, Jay's prospects for tomorrow, Anne and Vanessa, and life and the Universe. Then they crashed into a deep sleep.

At the point where he was in his deepest sleep, Dane had the craziest dream. It was set in some ancient time when kings lived in giant castles and anyone who dared to speak against them or the church was struck down without mercy.

He saw a wizard being taken before some kind of hearing. He was in chains for he had dared to speak about that of which speech was forbidden. He had spoken of the spirit world and the forces of nature, and now it was time to pay the price.

The air was damp and heavy with terror. The wizard knew the Church wanted to vent their religious fury on him. He had been found guilty of contradicting their teachings and even though what he said was true, he knew that he would be dead by morning. The wizard felt great sorrow and betrayal in his heart and yet he was defiant as he uttered his last words:

"You can deny man's nature here on Earth but the wrath of the gods shall fall upon you."

Dane woke with a start, he looked at his digital clock and saw that it was 4.44am. 'Wow, that was heavy' he thought, lying still and wide awake for the next half hour. He felt the dream was a real memory of his own past life in which he had been the wizard. What's more, he felt his passion for the truth, here and now, was somehow connected to that past.

Jay had done Avondale and Australia proud. He ended up being chaired up the beach and as he came past, Darren gave him his sponsor's hat for the presentation, reminding him how pleased Natural Rhythm would be that *their* boy got second in *their* contest.

A crowd of local supporters gathered around Jay. Everyone from the local Boardriders Club was there, plus his parents and heaps of his mates. They all congratulated Jay who now had a smile like a split watermelon. He put on his sponsor's cap and turned towards the stage.

It was time for Dane and Vanessa to rally the troops for a chat with Doug Toovey after the presentation. Dane was amazed as they had over four hundred signatures, a number any politician would surely take seriously.

Like most other events, the Natural Rhythm Pro had a quick on beach presentation, to be followed by an Awards Dinner that night. Doug Toovey thought it would be good publicity to present the winner's cheque on Avo beach in front of an adoring crowd. The crowd gave a big cheer for Ricardo Molina who kissed the cross around his neck and saluted the crowd.

The loudest applause came for Jay. Doug Toovey, always happy to align himself with anything or anyone popular, described Jay as *'Our boy from Avondale.'* Jay made a really good speech,

"I'd like to thank my coach Darren Connors, my family and all my friends, ...and... I'd like to thank Natural Rhythm for running a great event and everyone for coming down to watch. Oh, and I'd like to thank the judges, except the ones in the final."

The crowd laughed with delight at their home town finalist.

After the presentation Jay was walking with a group of people that included Molina and Doug Toovey and his *minder.* As the contest crowd was dispersing, a new crowd was gathering behind Dane Capper, aiming to head off Jay and the others.

"Excuse me sir, we would all like to present you with something," said Dane Capper politely as he stood in front of Doug Toovey.

"Well that depends on what it is?" said Toovey, causing those around him to laugh.

"It's a Petition sir. It's something we'd really like you to look at sir, if you could just watch this movie and talk to us about it, you know, as our elected representative."

Jay was proud of the way Dane spoke, while Molina looked confused by what was going on.

"Well what's the movie about? asked Doug Toovey cautiously.

"Fluoride sir, this movie says its toxic waste, they even say that in America, babies are not allowed to be bottle fed with it. We want to know about this, that's all." Dane was firm but respectful.

Toovey was silent for a moment. He hadn't got to where he was without deadly rat cunning and he tried to confuse Dane.

"How do I even know this movie is true?" he asked Dane aggressively.

"I have hundreds of signatures sir, over four hundred in fact, couldn't you just watch the movie. It's actually pretty interesting."

"Yeah," said someone in the crowd. "Just watch the movie Toovey," yelled someone else.

"But I don't even know it's true?" Toovey stuck to his guns and so it was becoming a ridiculous stand-off.

"We can't let you go until you agree sir," said Dane, as a joke and to lighten the mood.

Felton Ross was no ordinary *minder;* that was why he charged top dollar to look out for Doug Toovey.

"What do you mean you can't let us go?" he said to Dane threateningly, and then he began typing a text message.

The crowd started to boo and jeer, drowning out Dane's reply to Felton. "Hey it was only a joke sir, no disrespect...please sir, just take the petition," Dane pleaded.

"I don't even know if it's true," snarled Toovey.

The crowd were booing and jeering at Doug Toovey. And then the kids began to chant in unison, *'watch the movie Toovey, watch the movie Toovey,'* over and over. Dane thought this was funny until

111

two police cars arrived. The police began to disperse the crowd, but Dane was escorted into a squad car and taken to the Police Station, much to everyone's horror.

Felton made a mental note to tell the newspapers to mention Doug's impeccable behaviour and fantastic people skills, and how he defused the situation like the wise and compassionate man he is. Yeah that sounds about right he thought to himself with a smile.

Felton was comfortable that the situation had been neutralized, although he would have preferred to rough Dane up, just to show him who he was dealing with. He would also need to do the usual background checks into the ringleaders of this little circus. He and Doug hopped into his car and drove away as the police followed with Dane in the back.

The crowd stood in stunned silence.

"He'll be right," said Darren, "it's not like they're going to charge him are they?"

"I don't know," said Jay, "this is totally bogus." Jay convinced Darren to drive to Avondale Police Station to try to speak to the Duty Sergeant.

The Sergeant congratulated Jay on his results and told him that Mr Toovey would not be taking any further action. They would release Dane as soon as an adult in his family collected him.

"The thing is, his oldies are away and so is his big brother Simon," said Jay, "so who is going to sign Dane out?"

"There's not much you can do champ," said Sergeant Hunter, "we have already made calls to his brother and sister. We know the family but we have to do it by the book, especially when a politician has been involved."

34

The morning after

The next morning, Jay sat on his veranda eating some berries with yoghurt. He was still processing what had happened the day before. His second place in the Natural Rhythm Pro was his biggest ever result by a mile, second in a world tour event while he was still in school.

He had really enjoyed the Presentation Party, Darren and a few of the older guys from the Boardriders Club were pretty drunk and as he didn't drink alcohol, it was really funny watching them. Everyone had been so pleased to see a local boy crack the big time, and accordingly the energy was really positive. To be honest though, Jay wasn't comfortable until Dane finally arrived a few hours late.

Jay had already shrugged off the incident at the beach. He saw nothing wrong with what Dane had done. What's wrong with being so enthusiastic about the truth. Who wouldn't complain about toxic waste in our water, and Doug Toovey had acted like a little weasel, dodging Dane's simple requests. He saw it with his own eyes.

'Fair dinkum,' thought Jay, 'give a bloke a go, he was asking questions on behalf of all teenagers in the Avondale Shire.' Jay wished they would interview him on National News now, he'd set the buggers straight.

A number of the pros, including Rob Slade, had told Jay that they thought it was cool that the teenagers wanted some answers. They also told him there was lots of opposition to water fluoridation in other parts of the world.

Later that morning, when Jay walked onto the school quadrangle it was high fives all round. His good mates, and then lots of other kids, congratulated him on his success.

"Thirty grand Jay, that's not a bad day's work for a kid from Avondale," said Barry Hobbs.

Jacob Vaughan spoke sarcastically, "I can't believe you got second bra, what happened?" He gave Jay a quick punch to the ribs and then continued, "we're not gonna treat you any different now that your famous."

Jay felt good to be the centre of such heartfelt good wishes.

"Has anyone seen Crapper?" Barry Hobbs asked, "I haven't heard from him since the ruckus yesterday."

"Yeah, I saw him last night, he made it to the party when he got out of gaol." Jay spoke with pride.

As it happened, Dane was running late for school, arriving just before the bell, to rousing cheers from his mates. Word had spread like wildfire and Dane was the new mouthpiece of teenage angst. Reluctantly, the boys set off for Economics.

Dane told the boys that he thought it best not to mention what happened to Miss Stevens, unless she already knew of course.

"We want her to keep letting us do our own thing and yesterday might just freak her out a bit." he told the others wisely.

"Good point," said Barry, "let's pass the word around."

"Hopefully, the only big news she hears is that Jay won thirty grand," said Dane and the others all nodded.

35

General Studies : Charlotte talks about food

Monday morning dawned like any other day for Crystal who had no inkling that a storm was coming her way. She was a little tired after returning late from her weekend away with Beth, but otherwise, it was business as usual. She and Beth had travelled down to Eden to visit her family. The weather had been divine and they had a lovely time. In no hurry to leave, they arrived home quite late on Sunday evening. Crystal had no idea about the fun and games at the beach the day before.

Charlotte Huntley couldn't understand why everyone wasn't vegetarian. She smiled broadly as Crystal introduced her and then surprised everyone with her light and informative style and her excellent technique. She started with an overview of her presentation.

We should all be vegetarian because it:
- Makes our food and water resources go so much further so they can help save people who are starving and dying of thirst, and stopping the so called need for genetic modification;
- Is so much kinder to animals;
- Is so much healthier (even for elite athletes);

- Makes a healthier society which spends much less on healthcare; and
- So many great people who we have considered to be leaders were also vegetarian.

She showed a quote from Albert Einstein:

'Nothing will benefit human health and increase the chances for survival of life on Earth as much as the evolution to a vegetarian diet.'

"Wow, talk about bringing out the big guns," said Hobbsy.

"That's right Barry," she said, "not just Einstein, but so many others in history who were considered enlightened or outstanding in some way, also favoured a vegetarian diet. Other examples included Leonardo da Vinci, Pythagoras and Gandhi. As for Einstein however, it seems amazing that such a strong opinion from one of our brightest intellects is not more widely known." 'Good point,' thought Crystal.

Charlotte then told the story of George Bernard Shaw, a famous writer who became a vegetarian at age 25. He did this against the stern warnings of his doctors. When asked many years later if he had gone back and told the doctors of his excellent health, he said *'I would but they are all dead.'* The class laughed, putting Charlotte even more at ease.

She put up a photo of a truckload of pigs. It was pretty obvious where they were going.

"Ivy has already spoken about cruelty and this photo says it all. Look at how squashed these poor piggies are, no doubt to save transport costs. Why kill these creatures when we don't even need to?

As for the health benefits," said Charlotte, "where do I begin? Even dating back to 1961, the Journal of the American Medical Association argued that a vegetarian diet could prevent more than half the deaths caused by heart disease. They were talking about a

50% decrease in our biggest killer, it amazes me that this is not more widely known." said Charlotte.

'I have to agree,' thought Crystal.

Charlotte then showed a clip from a movie called *Forks over Knives* discussing an incredible study on cancer commissioned in 1974 by Chinese Premier Zhou Enlai, after he was diagnosed with terminal bladder cancer.

"Can you believe it?" said Charlotte. "On finding out about his illness, this incredible leader commissioned a study to give his country a more complete understanding of cancer."

This study was by far the largest of its kind ever undertaken. After years of painstaking analysis, they produced a very detailed cancer map for China. Later, American and Chinese doctors combined to produce a detailed study of this information, showing 94,000 correlations between what you eat and disease.

FORKS OVER KNIVES

"Like any truth," said Charlotte, "those who don't like it will try to question the science, but the New York Times called the China Study the most comprehensive study ever undertaken of the relationship between diet and the risk of disease and the findings are very clear. The studies clearly show that a lower percentage of people on a plant-based diet die from cancer, stroke and heart disease, than those who eat animals."

"You just wonder why this stuff is not more widely known," said Warren Longbottom.

"The good news," said a smiling Charlotte, "it finally seems to be sinking in."

She clicked on the *Forks over Knives* website and showed an endorsement of the movie by Academy award winning director James Cameron, who directed Titanic, Terminator and Avatar. Mr. Cameron said he is feeling healthier and has more endurance since changing to a plant based diet. He is obviously passionate about this, saying that

> *'You can't be an environmentalist, you can't be an ocean steward without truly walking the walk; and you can't walk the walk in the world of the future, the world ahead of us, the world of our children, not eating a plant-based diet.'*

THE CHINA STUDY

"Terminate meat eaters," joked Jay, in reference to Cameron's most famous character.

'It's amazing how people take words more seriously when a famous person says them,' thought Crystal.

Charlotte then played a segment on Mac Danzig, an Ultimate Fighting Champion who is a vegan. As Mac said, 'Most people think vegetarians are all hippies but that is not the case.' This point was obvious to the class as they watched Mac's incredible fitness and strength, and his aggression in the ring.

In fact, he went on a twelve fight winning streak immediately after becoming vegan, dispelling the myth that if you are an athlete, you need animal protein. Crystal could see that this segment really caught the attention of the boys, who obviously looked up to UFC athletes.

"That dude is a machine," said Jacob. "A vegan mean machine," said Hobbsy.

MAC DANZIG

Crystal was impressed at how Charlotte was putting this forward rationally, using great statistics and real people, to support vegetarianism. She then raised genetically modified foods, and pesticides, as another example of people living in total ignorance about what they were eating.

"Testing of GM foods has shown a great deal to worry about," said Charlotte.

"Despite this, the Government says foods don't have to say whether they include GM ingredients on the label and so despite the dangers, it's hard for people to choose not to eat them. They are experimenting on us without our consent," there was contempt in Charlotte's voice.

"Maybe," said Gemma Healey, "but who wants bugs on our foods anyway. Surely we need some pesticide?"

'Uh oh,' thought Crystal, 'here we go.'

Charlotte was intense enough to scare her teacher a little. She turned beetroot red, looked right at Gemma and almost screamed,

"When your grandchildren are all f...ing sterile, maybe they'll wish you thought a bit more about this Gemma."

"Charlotte, calm down. No swearing please. You are making a good point, can you do it without swearing."

"I'm sorry miss," said Charlotte.

"Thanks," said Crystal, "and please apologise to Gemma as well."

"I'm so sorry Gemma," said Charlotte sarcastically and then continued in a softer tone.

GMO STUDIES

"In some scientific GMO studies, in addition to the tumours in the first generation of test rats, many of their third generation offspring were sterile and useless and basically could not survive."

Even Mike Waters seemed confused by this.

"Charlotte, doesn't our whole lab testing system assume that humans have similar reactions to animals. In my opinion, that's why they test things and say they are safe if animals aren't hurt. Just like Ivy explained, it's really cruel but isn't that why they do it?"

"Exactly Mike. Hello. The animals are getting sterile in only three generations. Even though many scientists have spoken against ignoring these results, that's basically what we do."

The class was stunned and Charlotte continued.

"So I personally find this frustrating but hey we'll have to wait a few generations for the results of the experiments on us. If this also happens to humans, well, as bugs bunny would say .....that's all folks". Crystal herself was shocked about this.

"These GMO methods are said to give us more production, to save our resources. Well, it has been shown that it takes sixteen pounds of grain to make one pound of beef and that at least in a study in the US, a person switching to a vegetarian diet saves more water than if they gave up showering."

The class were obviously shocked about this.

"Isn't it obvious, we really do have the resources to feed starving people if we all choose to stop eating meat. It's a much better use of our resources, it's so much more humane and it makes us healthier. Everybody wins."

ENVIRONMENTAL BENEFITS OF VEGETARIANISM

"Except the meat and dairy industry," said Dane.

"Yeah and don't forget the drug companies, I guess they lose money if people are healthier," said Warren Longbottom.

As suggested by her parents when she practiced her talk, Charlotte was determined to finish on a positive note. She spoke enthusiastically about the massive resurgence in organic farming occurring in India, shown in the movie *One Man, One Cow, One Planet.*

They say now that cow manure is a far superior fertilizer than the chemical ones, and it enhances the soil rather than destroying it. So many farmers in India are going back to the ancient natural farming methods that sustained them and their lands for many thousands of years, before they were tricked into using chemicals.

I think I understand one reason why cows are sacred in India," Charlotte said, "it's their manure."

Charlotte smiled, "thank you for listening."

The class burst into applause.

"That was fantastic Charlotte," said Crystal, clearly impressed, "feeding all the starving people in the world is a very noble goal. Let's hope people wake up to this." As Crystal spoke these words, she thought about changing her own eating habits.

"They will miss, the *end of illusion* is coming soon," said Tina cryptically, as the bell rang to end another stimulating class.

ONE MAN ONE COW ONE PLANET

36

Another dinner at Gemma's

Gemma Healey planned to talk to her father again that evening at dinner. He wasn't a cancer specialist but surely he will know about heart disease she thought, it's our biggest killer and he is a really good doctor.

She had made notes about what Charlotte said. Even back in 1961 they already knew that half the deaths caused by heart disease could be prevented by a vegetarian diet. How could they know this and not do it thought Gemma, understanding now what Ivy and Charlotte were saying.

Gemma had easily found statistics showing that in America over 616,000 people died of heart disease in 2008; 25% of all deaths. It was the leading cause of death for both men and women. The situation in Australia was just as grim, heart disease also killed over 50,000 people in 2008.

Gemma heard her mum call her for dinner so she grabbed her folder and headed for the dining room. Walking in to find her parents seated, Gemma placed her folder on the sideboard and sat down to her meal. It was a delicious pasta with a rich creamy sauce and pine nuts and bacon. They talked as they ate, Gemma waiting for the right moment to show off what she had learned.

"Dad," she said "what if somebody could reduce heart disease by half?"

"Heart disease is our biggest killer darling, I'd say that sort of a reduction would be mighty unbelievable."

"There are plenty of things you can do dad, not just eliminating animal fats but even things like eating cayenne pepper, a herb that stimulates and strengthens the heart. People showing symptoms could look at a checklist of natural things for prevention, in the case of heart symptoms, they could be told to take regular cayenne pepper, or even magnesium which also helps the heart."

Gemma was obviously excited about this, and continued stating her case, "I find this really interesting and with respect dad, it seems like the doctors do a great job of fixing the problems, that's their job of course, but what about prevention? It doesn't seem like the system has enough focus on prevention." She knew from her research that this made sense.

Rupert's nostrils flared and he glared at his daughter. "Just where are you getting this crap from?"

"We are talking about this in General Studies dad. We have a fantastic teacher, I told you remember, Miss Stevens, it's really interesting."

"Just what the hell are they teaching the kids these days? What makes Miss Stevens qualified to talk about this?"

After dinner, Rupert made a note in his diary to remind him to call Trevor Rawles, an old mate of his who was Deputy Principal of Avondale High.

37

Gathering of the troops

Craig had been handed the note which was passed around during Crystal's class. Nothing too detailed, just an invitation from Dane to the class.

> *Everyone who wants to support Teenagers for Truth is welcome at my house at 7 o'clock sharp. No need to bring anything. No adults allowed.*

Craig decided to go to Dane's and find out how he could help. Most of the others in the class made the same decision and what's more, because the note said everyone was welcome, most students told their friends.

Later, as he and Vanessa discussed their plans for the evening, Craig realised that they were heading off to the same gathering. He understood why Vanessa had deliberately kept quiet about Teen's for Truth. Her parents let her run around with anyone she wanted, but that would change with the first hint of more rebellious behaviour.

Craig was obviously not expecting Vanessa to be hanging out with Dane, and so, he was taken aback at first when she mentioned going to the gathering and told him about Anne's party.

On reflection he realised that nothing would surprise him about his sister. A butterfly could flap its wings and she'd be dating Zac Efron, so why not Dane Capper?

"Dane is one of the dudes who put the water bomb that soaked me on the fans," said Craig, "but he's a nice guy, even gave me his towel to dry off."

"It's a small world," said Vanessa. "Wait until you see his house."

'Of course,' thought Craig, 'my younger sister had already seen Dane's house.'

Vanessa could not resist reminding Craig that it had been a while since he socialized.

"It's different at this school," said Craig, not mentioning that the whole class had been invited.

"Welcome to the new Craig," she teased "or maybe they just like nerds?"

They bickered good naturedly right up until their mum dropped them at Dane's. There was already quite a crowd. Most of Crystal's class including Jay, of course, Jacob, Hobbsy, Tina, Gemma, Naomi, Warren Longbottom, Ivy, and even Albert.

Dane directed everyone to the massive courtyard which could handle quite a crowd. Craig walked in with Vanessa,

"I believe you know my sister."

"Wow," said Dane, slightly embarrassed about being with Craig's younger sister, "you guys don't look alike at all."

Craig left Dane and Vanessa and walked over to join the others. He could see that Mike Waters was deep in conversation with Jacob, Barry and Jay, who were enthusiastically picking his brain, hoping to apply his genius to their plans.

The Super Nerd didn't disappoint, suggesting a website which included online petitions and polling on different topics, a *fortress* of some kind with full system replication.

"This means if anyone ever crashes our system, we will have immediate back-up."

"Nice plan Sergeant Nerdsworth," said Jay light-heartedly.

Like some kind of teenage Union Movement, the group

formulated plans and schemes and schemes and plans. They agreed they would firstly continue to push the petition with Doug Toovey, and keep getting more and more signatures every day, even from oldies as well.

A few kids suggested they write a letter to the local press explaining about the incident and the petition.

"All in favour," said Hobbsy, sounding like a union boss.

Dane had become a bit of a celebrity after his run in with Doug Toovey. Those teenagers who saw what happened at the beach spread the word. They knew that Dane was polite and respectful and they thought it was stupid that Doug Toovey didn't just agree to watch the movie and update them about the issues they have raised. Truth be told, they felt a bit disgruntled, what was he hiding and why should Dane get taken away in a police car?

The teens were puzzled that the press reported it as if they were at fault. This made the kids even angrier. If Doug Toovey had simply honoured their reasonable polite request, there would not have been a problem.

They talked about other ways they could make a difference, after all, they already had a readymade network.

"Hundreds of teenagers at the push of a button and in my opinion," said the super nerd, "this could easily become thousands."

"If we all stick together," said Dane "we could really show them we mean business. We just want the truth but we need them to take us seriously."

"Here here," said Hobbsy and then adding, as if thinking aloud,

"What if we all agreed on a certain thing, like nobody buy particular products from big companies unless Doug gives us our answers? It could be powerful if we all did it."

Dane responded excitedly, "great idea, I bet we get noticed then."

"We can do it across the Globe," said Craig, already talking big.

"We can get a lead person in every country, it would be sick. Can your programs replicate in each country?" he asked Mike seriously.

"Absolutely," replied the super nerd, clearly enjoying the question.

Craig was showing a hidden side, he could take control and make things happen. Listening to them all talk in the glorified atmosphere of the stately manor courtyard, the students obviously saw the potential for this to go right around the globe.

The Group, with mainly Dane, Mike and Craig actually talking, mapped out a strategy. They believed that Teenagers for Truth had the ability to achieve results through their numbers and cooperation.

Suggestions included:

- Do petitions and online polling;
- Have a *fun* website, which also simply explains the petition, with some links;
- Research to support the arguments e.g. the research paper against fluoride which is endorsed by three thousand professionals;
- Research on which other countries stopped fluoride;
- Explore other areas where the truth is hidden, like free energy and GMO Foods.

"Perhaps we could even start a *true* newspaper?" said Jacob "Just look at what they said about Sunday, their story is not even close."

"Our parents accept the lies but we won't," said Dane. "We simply can't." Everyone cheered. The crowd were excited by this fun cause and everyone loved being at the stately manor. The conversation continued enthusiastically for a few hours.

"We should also look at this fracking," said Albert. "The elders are very worried about it, the water spirits have told them that it will be a big problem, these fellas think they're clever getting the gas out and selling it, but they are using lots of poisons to get it and they stay in the water. The only thing clever is the way they trick people to think its ok. There is a big rally coming up, I think we all should go."

Barry Hobbs looked at his brothers and rolled his eyes,

"Oh no, not here as well, this is happening back home now and causing all sorts of problems. Barry now knew what he would be doing his assignment on, it would be a good excuse to contact his relatives back home.

"Same thing in America," said Ivy. "I saw a movie called Gasland, the people that lived near the wells could actually light a match near their tap water and the water would catch on fire, it's just so…" she was lost for words and had tears in her eyes.

"Don't worry Ivy, we'll get onto that as well," said Jay reassuringly, he too had a soft spot for this lovely gentle soul.

"We sure will," said Dane. "So much to do and so little time," he spoke in a funny voice, waving his hands in the air. Speaking of time, we should probably call it a night."

You have set a really good platform tonight, thanks mate," said Jay genuinely and as he started to clap his hands, everyone joined in to show their gratitude for Dane.

Craig was really pleased about the night. He could sense that there was lots of scope for him to use his skills and they had a pretty good team of people involved.

"Hey big brother, you were really good tonight," Vanessa told him as they waited for a lift home.

"All you need now is some cool clothes and a new haircut."

38

Crystal and Beth

During and after dinner, Crystal had spent hours listening to what was going on in Beth's life. She heard all about Adam, Beth's latest client from her personal training, who was also now officially her latest 'crush.' Beth was agonizing over how to weigh her personal needs against her professional duty.

Crystal couldn't resist telling Beth about Charlotte's presentation and simply that everyone was still participating in the class discussions. She was really proud of 'her' kids.

"You know what, I am actually learning from the kids. Beth, I bet you can't guess who said:

> *"Nothing will benefit human health and increase the chances for survival of life on Earth as much as the evolution to a vegetarian diet"*

Beth had no real inspiration, she knew it must be someone famous so she said 'Sting,' which was actually not a bad guess, as he is a pretty well know 'alternative' person.

"It was none other than Albert Einstein," said Crystal proudly. "Not to mention that Gandhi, Pythagoras and Leonardo da Vinci were all vegetarian as well."

"Wow," said Beth. "That is so great, because I am thinking of giving up meat. Adam is a vegetarian," she added proudly.

"No Beth, it's so amazing because some of the most famous brilliant innovative people in history were vegetarian, and I only learned this because of my students. The kids are so amazing." Crystal was one very proud teacher.

39

Watching Dane

Felton Ross read the report on Dane Capper. Apart from the disturbance at the beach, it said that Capper had been searching websites they didn't like. Ones that told the truth about free energy, fluoride and other areas that needed to be strictly controlled. There were also lots of recent viewings of a protest clip Mr Capper was in.

He was definitely a troublemaker and was marked as a *potential person of influence*. 'We'll have to keep an eye on you matey,' he said softly to himself.

40

General Studies : Albert on reconnecting with nature

Crystal introduced Albert Rose as the class applauded enthusiastically. He had already moved the kids during the group discussions and they were all eager to hear what he had in mind to fix the planet. His first slide summarised what he thought was needed.

Mankind simply has to reconnect with nature.

"The white man," he said smiling broadly, "oops, I mean modern man is pretty much cut off from nature. Our elders tell stories about times when people had a spiritual connection with nature.

They tell us of the hunt. Three or four hunters would all spear only the eldest or sickest animal of the herd. It wasn't just the hunters, many in the tribe would participate by preparing the meal or even using the bones and hide. Nothing went to waste. The tribe would honour the animal's contribution to the web of life. It was a time far removed from today's inhuman treatment of the creatures we eat.

Many indigenous people around the world are also suffering because they too have lost their connection with nature. Society tries to convert them to the white man's ways but those ways know no such connection, so they resist. Many are lost and so is mankind as a whole, unless we reconnect with nature."

Crystal was impressed by this point. "Are you saying that our whole society seems disconnected, just like indigenous people who no longer live in their true connection with nature?"

"Yes Miss Stevens," he said modestly. "The scientists talk about *survival of the fittest* but it is ignorant to apply this to particular people. It should be survival of the *fittingest,* meaning that mankind as a species will only survive if he fits in better and cooperates with his environment."

SURVIVAL OF THE FITTINGEST

"That is a very good point Albert, well done." said Crystal.

The modest young man at the front of the room then showed a film clip about an experiment where children had a running race for a prize which was a basket of fruit.

In America, the kids raced and the winner took the fruit.

In Africa, the kids all joined hands as they ran and then shared the fruit.

The power of this clip was just incredible.

"This sharing must be the way of the future," he said.

Albert spoke of the Native Americans who his tribe considered as brothers. He showed a famous quote about the damage money does.

'When all the trees have been cut down,
when all the animals have been hunted,
when all the waters are polluted,
when all the air is unsafe to breathe,
only then will you discover you cannot eat money.'

"I have heard my mother say those exact words," said Tina. "She says we must again connect with nature and each other, to bring *oneness* to the planet."

"That's very holistic Tina, is your mother still a doctor?" As Crystal asked this question, a number of students froze.

"No Miss," said Tina, "my mum died last June."

"Oh Tina, I am so sorry to hear that." Crystal felt embarrassed.

"Please don't feel bad Miss, I understand the journey of life and death," said Tina "and I cherish what she has told me." Crystal made a note to talk to Tina's dad as she was saying some pretty unusual things and Crystal wondered if her dad should know about this.

Albert had another great quote, this time from a letter written by Chief Seattle, a Susquamish chief, responding to the American President who wanted to buy his tribe's land.

> *"Will you teach your children what we have taught our children? That the Earth is our mother. That what befalls the Earth befalls all the sons of the Earth.*
>
> *This we know: the Earth does not belong to man, man belongs to the Earth.*
>
> *All things are connected like the blood that unites us all. Humankind has not woven the web of life. We are but one thread within it. Whatever we do to the web, we do to ourselves. All things are bound together. All things connect. We are a part of the Earth and it is part of us."*

"Everyone should read this great Chief's wisdom," said Albert.

"Everything is energy, but man does not see energy," he continued, "he sees only money and what his scientists can measure. He misses the miracles of the universe."

"That is so profound Albert, thank you." Crystal was moved by his words.

"I agree Albert," said Mike Waters, "money does get in the way, but the connection between all things has now definitely been scientifically proven. We are all part of one big hologram."

CHIEF SEATTLE

"Please explain?" joked Jacob, rolling his eyes at Mike.

"Well, say for example you have a holographic image of a rose, and you cut off a small part and then look at that part with a magnifying glass, you will still see the whole rose."

"So that is why they say we are all one, wow, I get it," said Jacob gratefully.

Albert continued, "maybe the scientists can now say this, Mike and I thank you for explaining, but so what, we don't live it. If we did, we would never harm nature because we could see that we are harming ourselves.

Our society ignores this connection with nature but it's all around us. Remember the Boxing Day Tsunami? Did you know that the elephants all walked to higher ground? How did they know what was coming?"

"Just like when someone's dog is waiting at the door for them before they get home," said Ivy Watkins.

"Exactly," said Mike "in fact, a leading scientist named Rupert Sheldrake has done video experiments on this, with lots of dog owners driving their cars. An owner would be randomly called and told to head home and at *that* moment, their dog was filmed getting up and going to the door. Time and time again, the dogs moved when the car was turning around. It shows that our minds are connected, or entangled as Dr Sheldrake puts it."

RUPERT SHELDRAKE

"Just like when you are about to phone someone and they call you," said Crystal, fascinated by the discussion.

She looked at Albert and got the impression that he didn't mind everyone talking. He seemed pleased to have initiated a discussion for so many people.

"It's like we are tapped into each other," said Jacob.

"So that's why they say it's powerful if lots of people meditate together," said Craig Sceats intensely.

It was as if Tina had a sudden brainwave, "What if everyone in the world, or at least, lots of people had a day of connection between themselves and the Earth, all at the same time?"

"Well," said Albert "that would bring great joy to Mother Earth. She is alive you know. Next time you are out in nature, try to consciously connect with mother Earth or with the trees or the ocean. Next time you are eating a meal, try to feel gratitude to nature for providing it for you."

These words, spoken with reverence by Albert, were a fitting end to his presentation.

Crystal thanked Albert and everyone gave him a round of applause.

THE POWER OF MEDITATION

GRATITUDE

After the class, Crystal called Tina's father at his work and arranged to meet on Friday afternoon. She felt better once she had made the appointment, if nothing else, she wanted to apologise again to Tina in front of her dad.

41

Mike Water's place

Dane Capper spent Friday afternoon at Mike's place with Ivy, Craig, Barry and Tina, getting things organized for Teens for Truth. There were lots of areas of life where teenagers needed answers. Just what are the adults doing with the world? It's almost like they don't even care.

As well as fluoride in the water, other things worth investigating were new energy, GMO foods and farming without chemicals.

Mike was a programming genius and the project had given him a sense of purpose. It had connected him with other kids, his favourite being Ivy. As the group listened intently, he presented his ideas for cutting edge software for Teens for Truth, explaining how he would create a full back up system with a separate cyber identity.

It was likely their system would be hacked if adults became aware of what they were doing so it was better to anticipate this and create a fool proof defence.

"So you are saying that if they hack us, the system will simply replicate and the old system will lead them in circles while we continue as if nothing had happened." Barry Hobbs was clearly impressed.

"But won't the systems have the same internet id?" asked Craig.

"Yes and no," said Mike enigmatically. "You see, there will be layers of access and only those we approve will be able to get into the actual system. Others, undesirables shall we call them, will think they are in but they won't be. In my opinion, it's well worth the trouble to create it that way."

"That's brilliant Mike," said Ivy, flashing him her lovely smile.

Mike's mum came to the door with a jug of lemonade and a plate of her home made banana bread.

"I thought you could do with a break," she said kindly, taking turns to serve them.

"This is delicious Mrs Waters," said Dane, ever polite. As they ate the boys discussed ways to get Teens for Truth going in a number of countries at once.

Tina and Ivy had their own conversation about Tina's idea for a *'Teenage Earth Day.'*

"I wish you could see what I see. What I have always been able to see. Devas, fairies, nature spirits, elves, they are here to help us if we would only ask them. Man accepted the role of tending the Earth but rejects the gifts given for this purpose." There was sadness in Ivy's voice.

"Tina, do you know about Findhorn?"

"No Ivy, but please tell me."

"*Findhorn* is a wonderful story that most people would never believe, but it's true, it's been documented. During the 1970's a couple were *guided* to contact and cooperate with nature spirits and devas. With the help of these spirits, and lots of hard work, they grew incredible trees, flowers and vegetables on windswept barren sand dunes in the north of Scotland. It shows just how powerful the nature spirits are.

The spirits say they just want to help us and have fun, and they are sad because humans are taught that they are not real. We have so many problems with our food, and yet, we ignore those who were sent to help us. We need to honour these spirits, tell them we believe in them and that we would love them to help us."

Tina could see that Ivy was really sad.

"Perhaps we, the teenagers, can all consciously try to connect with those spirits?" said Tina.

"Tina, I would love that and so would the nature spirits."

Ivy spoke from the heart and Tina could sense her joy at the prospect of this reconnection.

FINDHORN

42

The Skate Park

Jay Williams was right behind Teens for Truth. He knew he led a charmed life and was well aware that many others were not so lucky. He was surprised by what he had learnt so far and could see that we should all be making more effort to help the Earth.

After the end of another school week however, he really felt like getting some exercise rather than going to Mike's place. The waves were no good so he and Jacob were doing some skateboarding at the local skate park. Jay saw this as part of his training and he did it whenever he could.

They had been at the skate ramp for at least an hour when Jacob saw Anne and Vanessa riding past on their bikes. Jacob had told Anne she might be able to find him there, and he signalled to them to come over. While Anne and Jacob chatted, Vanessa watched as Jay rode his skateboard up and over the bowl, up off the lip and then down onto the flat. She knew a bit about skateboarding as her last boyfriend was a champion skateboarder. She could see that Jay had flair.

He stopped skating and walked over to join the others.

"G'day," he said, with a friendly chuckle.

"Wow, you're really good," said Vanessa. Her eyes seemed to sparkle right at him. She was a picture of radiant health, wearing only a bikini top and denim shorts. While Vanessa had not lived near the beach for long, with her platinum blonde hair and tanned skin, she looked very much the surfie girl.

"Geez it's pretty hot," said Jacob.

"Let's ride into town to get a nice cool drink. We can give you guys a double," Vanessa suggested hopefully, motioning to Anne and their bikes.

"Why not," said Jacob.

Minutes later, Jay was balanced on the seat of Vanessa's bike with his right arm around her bare midriff. He had to hang on quite firmly with his right hand as his left hand held his skateboard. Jay could feel the rhythm of Vanessa's body as she pushed the peddles up and down. Once they had finished the climb up Flinders Road, Vanessa relaxed and sat back against Jay as they cruised along Denman Avenue.

'This chick is something else,' he caught himself thinking. He wasn't worried about Dane because as far as he was concerned, he was just getting a double to the shops on a hot day, no big deal right? Maybe, maybe not, nevertheless, as soon as they stopped at Avondale Mall, Jay jumped straight off the back of Vanessa's bike.

"Thanks for the lift Vanessa," he said with a smile.

"My *pleasure* Jay," her tone was a little too friendly, 'wasn't she his best mate's girlfriend' he thought?

They sat talking and laughing and drinking their drinks.

"I wonder how the others are going at Mike's place," said Jay.

"Yeah who would have thought they'd all be hanging out at the super nerd's place," said Jacob.

"Teens for Truth is so cool," said Jay, "someone has to wake people up."

"I agree, Dane is such a cool guy and he is so great at getting people motivated," said Vanessa.

He sure is," said Jay, feeling an unfamiliar sensation of guilt and wondering what Dane would think if he could see him now.

43

Tommy meets the Teacher

Tommy was reading when the phone rang.

"Hi Tommy, you were right, I can't make the meeting with Tina's teacher, 3.00 pm on a Friday, what was I thinking? Sorry mate, I did try. Can you do me a huge favour and hear what she has to say?"

"No problem Mark, I'll just have to rearrange my busy schedule," said Tommy sarcastically. "Who do I ask for?"

"Miss Stevens, she's the teacher that Tina really likes. Call me if she needs my authority to speak to you about Tina."

"Too easy," said Tommy sensing Mark's relief that he could get back to his work.

"Oh and Tommy, no flirting with the teacher ok." Mark knew his younger brother well.

Tommy felt a sense of déjà vu as he walked up to the front office. He half expected the ladies to recognize him and was almost put out when they didn't.

"I am here to meet Miss Stevens," he said politely. As he waited, he was pleased to see a photo of his all-conquering School Rugby League team of 2003, sitting proudly on the wall. 'Wow,' he thought 'where did those nine years go?' He felt a slight sense of guilt at not having kept in touch with many of his old team mates.

"Mr. O'Brien?"

Tommy turned around and to his great surprise, he saw the *mystery girl* from the coffee shop standing in front of him. If anything, she was even more beautiful than he'd remembered. His heart raced as he tried hard to mask his great joy and relief at seeing her again.

"Well, yes and no… I'm Tommy, Tina's Uncle," he said barely keeping his composure. "Tina's dad was detained at the last minute. He is really sorry he couldn't make it and asked me to come."

Miss Stevens looked slightly taken aback so he clarified.

"It's ok, I live with them and truth be told, I spend a lot more time looking after Tina at the moment than her dad because he's really busy with his work. He said you can call him if you like."

"Ok, thank you Tommy, I'm Crystal Stevens, Tina's General Studies teacher." She took his hand and shook it warmly. "I have organized a meeting room, please follow me."

Tommy could not get over it. The *mystery girl* was Tina's teacher.

Crystal gestured to him to have a seat. She explained the situation and apologized about mentioning Tina's mum in class.

"That's understandable, how could you have known about Christine?" he replied in an understanding tone.

"Of course," she smiled and then continued, "look, I did want to apologize but the main reason I called Tina's dad was to discuss what Tina has been saying about her mother telling her things, after she has…..passed. Tina has said a few things which are kind of spooky but also quite interesting."

"I know about Tina's dreams," said Tommy, thinking that it was probably better for Tina that he was here instead of Mark.

Crystal explained that her best friend's older brother was an academic with expertise on the things that Tina had been talking about.

"Bradley is lovely and I've heard him talk about the ancient prophecies before. My feeling was that it would be helpful for Tina to chat with him. I mentioned it to him and he said we could call him now. I can go and get Tina if you like?"

"That's fine with me as long as it's fine with Tina." Tommy was feeling protective of his niece, as he should.

"I'll be back in a minute," said Crystal. As Tommy sat alone, he thought of Elliott's advice about the *mystery girl.*

> *"Thank the Universe for sending her to you. Then, simply act like you will see her again, and you will."*

Tommy had tried his best to do that every day since, and sure enough, he had seen her again. He was sitting in the meeting room about to have a conference call with her. He wished Elliott could see him now. 'Who knows, he probably can,' thought Tommy, still amazed by his contact with that unusual person, and excited that he had found his mystery girl.

Crystal returned with Tina and explained what she had in mind. "Is that ok with you Tina?" asked Tommy.

"Yeah sure Uncle Tommy, it sounds like fun," she replied. "OK, let's call him now," said Crystal excitedly.

Tommy loved her smile and still felt a familiarity with her that he could not explain. A million thoughts rushed through his head as she set up the call.

The office computer had webcam so she turned it around and put a chair for herself between Tina and Tommy. They could see Bradley and he could see them. Crystal made small talk with Bradley and then reminded him why she was calling and who she had with her. He was exceedingly pleasant as Tina told him some of the things her mother had said.

"Mum told me that:

> *"The Spiritual beings will remain to create one world and one nation under one power, that of the Creator."*

"That is what your mum said?" asked Bradley, raising his left eyebrow. He was very theatrical with his responses and he seemed a little sceptical.

"Those words are actually from a famous Indian Prophecy," he said and Tommy sensed that just like her father, Bradley may have thought that Tina was making it up as some kind of mechanism for coping with the loss of her mother.

"All of the ancients have foretold this and they say it's due to begin around the summer solstice." As if realizing the need to explain, Bradley clarified.

"There will be a very rare planetary alignment on 21 December to mark the coming changes. It's not the end of the world. The Mayans call it the end of time............ as we know it."

It was time for Tina to show Bradley how much she knew.

"We align with the galactic centre and the 'shoulder of the bull' in the constellation of Taurus, at roughly the galactic anti-centre. This is a time of great exaltation in the heavens," Tina beamed, "heralding the birth of a new galactic consciousness on Earth."

"Your mum said that? Man, that is awesome, it give me goose-bumps." Bradley spoke with great excitement.

"So Bradley, then it's not about destruction?" asked Tommy, still a little confused, "I mean, what about the apocalypse?"

"Do you actually know," said Bradley, "that apocalypse means…"

Tina cut in again, like lightning. "The lifting of the veils," she said triumphantly.

"Excellent." Bradley's admiration was obvious in his voice.

Tina continued, "mum said it's not about destruction, although it may take plenty of that to wake people up. It's about people seeing things the way they really are and working together for the greater good."

Bradley and Tina spoke to each other like two researchers working on the same science experiment and after a few more minutes, he seemed convinced. He stopped as if deep in thought and then asked her,

"Tina was your mum into this kind of thing before her passing?"

"Not that I know of, mum was a doctor," she replied, "and we have only ever spoken of this in my dreams, but she made it clear to me that teenagers need to wake up and understand the journey of life and death. If they do, they will see there is nothing to fear. Mum also said that we are pure and can help the Earth hold the new energies, if we choose to."

"I love that," said Bradley, he was revelling in the conversation and Tommy, listening intently and trying to keep up, felt very proud of his niece.

"There are many different descriptions of the Earth's evolution but essentially, they all say the same thing. I like the way the Incas put it, they say *"It's the Age of Meeting Ourselves Again."*

"Exactly," said Tina, "it's all about humans evolving, becoming connected to ourselves, to the Earth, to everyone and everything."

Bradley had heard enough.

"I must say Tina, your words, well your mother's words, accord exactly with ancient prophecies. There will indeed be exaltation in the heavens. *The Great Alignment* will signify the start of a new period of higher human consciousness. Personally, I think it will happen gradually over a number of years but of course, nobody knows for sure. It will happen however, as evolution is nature's way.

All of the ancient's foretold this in their own particular way and the Mayans showed it in their calendars. We cannot overstate its significance, and now it's here."

"So what you are saying Bradley is that Tina's mum's suggestions are accurate predictions of the future?"

"It's not so much a prediction, more of a message...*hello teenagers, your stupid parents and uncles, no offence Tommy, haven't thought of listening to the wisdom of the ancients, but maybe you should?"*

"I love it. Teenagers are here to wake up too. If their adult driven society doesn't facilitate it, they will do it themselves anyway. Tina has obviously volunteered to be some kind of catalyst."

Tina broke into a huge grin. She and Bradley were like kindred spirits and she seemed very pleased that he was honouring what her mum had told her.

Tommy found this subject fascinating and he was also a little embarrassed by his ignorance. "So how come we don't hear more about this Bradley, I mean, most people think of 2012 as some kind of prophecy that the world will end, and to be honest, the media makes it all sound pretty silly."

"Ah yes, the media. That is another conversation entirely Tommy, I'd be glad to discuss it sometime if you have about five spare hours, but for now, can I just say that people waking up is, well, it's bad for business."

"Wow, that is really interesting," Tommy spoke with great sincerity.

"My pleasure Tommy, you should be proud of Tina. I think she's right on the ball," said Bradley, "and I wish there were more young ones like her on the planet."

"I agree," said Crystal, "after hearing Tina and Bradley, it does all seem more real to me. I am interested to learn more about all of this."

"Excuse me, Bradley, can I ask something quickly before you go?" asked Tina.

"Of course," he said enthusiastically.

"We are thinking of getting lots of teenagers to all honour the Earth at the same time, like a teenager Earth Day or something. Someone told me that if more people think of something together, at once, it's more powerful. What do you think of this?" Tina obviously respected Bradley's opinion.

"It's perfect Tina, there is lots of evidence about how powerful group intentions are." Again he raised his left eyebrow, "are you sure you haven't been here before?"

"Well, not that I can remember," said Tina laughing.

Bradley got the joke and laughed along with her.

"The thing is," he said, "as a group, we usually only think about bad things. Like when people watch the news every night, they all see the bad stuff and think of it at the same time, so that group negativity, creates more bad stuff."

"I see what you mean," said Tommy. It made great sense and

really got him thinking, he had heard people say that our thoughts create our reality.

"Can I ask something, why does Christine come through in Tina's dreams?" asked Tommy.

"Good question Tommy, but it's really very simple. When we dream we go through various stages, different brainwaves as it were. When we reach the slower more relaxed states such as the theta brainwaves of R.E.M sleep, we are much more open to contact of this kind.

You probably get all sorts of messages and go to all kinds of places too, it's just that Tina can remember hers, that's all. Perhaps you should have a pen and paper next to your bed and write down your thoughts as soon as you wake up, like I do."

"Amazing," was all that Tommy could manage.

"Ok thanks Brad, we really appreciate your time," said Crystal.

"My pleasure," he said.

Crystal smiled warmly as she ended the call.

"What can I say Tina, I am just blown away," she said humbly.

Tina felt vindicated. "See Uncle Tommy, I told you my dreams were real."

"I'm really glad we made that call Miss Stevens," said Tommy enthusiastically, "it looks to me like my niece has it more together than anyone."

"Please call me Crystal. You are right, there's no need to worry, well maybe about our world but not about Tina." As Crystal spoke, she made eye contact with Tommy and he was momentarily lost in her emerald green eyes.

He tried to keep it formal as Mark's warning about flirting was still ringing in his ears.

"Keep up the good work, Tina has been really enthused about your classes." He felt that Crystal was partly responsible for the big change in Tina this year and he was sincerely grateful.

"Thanks Tommy." He could see from her expression that she really appreciated his compliment.

Tina had been thrilled about the meeting and once they were outside the school she showed her enthusiasm, "see Uncle Tommy, I told you Miss Stevens is really cool."

"Oh she's cool alright," said Tommy wondering whether he should tell Tina that Miss Stevens was the *mystery girl.*

44

The calm before the storm

In the short time she had been teaching, Crystal had empowered her students greatly. Far more in fact than she could ever imagine. She was still blissfully unaware of what she had unwittingly inspired Dane and his followers to do. Just by thinking outside the box and allowing them to choose their own topics and also by making them aware of movies like Thrive, Crystal had started a chain reaction.

She had no idea that things were about to really heat up for the kids and for her. Had she known, she may have cautioned the kids to take things slowly. After all, she wanted them to be able to think for themselves but she didn't want any trouble.

That night, she excitedly recounted her day to Beth. Beth was delighted to hear about Bradley. She was a bit of a revolutionary and it was her movies that had gotten Crystal's students moving in this direction.

"Tell me more about Bradley, is he hot?" asked Beth. She was on the lookout again as things had not gone so well with Adam, especially when she found out that he was actually married.

Crystal had decided not to tell Beth that she thought Tommy was really nice. After all, she had already made the mistake of mentioning Jay to Beth and she cringed every time Beth asked her about the hot guy from the beach. Just my luck she thought, a student's relative is almost as *off* limits as a student, especially when I met him through school.

'Can't I meet someone who has no links to Avondale High?' she thought.

45

General Studies: Barry talks about Fracking

Crystal could already tell that Barry Hobbs was a really popular kid but even she was surprised by the rousing reception the students gave him. He had obviously made quite an impression since moving over from London. He was Mr Personality and she was sure he would give an entertaining presentation.

"The world would be a better place if the oil companies allowed us to use cleaner energy," he began. "I know the technologies are there after watching Thrive but that's only because of Miss Stevens, otherwise, I'd be like all the people out there. They deserve to have hope for a better future but they simply don't get the information.

What we do to our planet is madness," continued Barry.

"Today I'll be talking about the latest example of this stupidity, 'Hydraulic fracturing' or 'fracking'. They pour tons of water, containing thousands of chemicals, into the ground until it literally fractures. The gas escapes through the cracks and they capture what they can and they say it's all ok. Where do they think the toxic water goes?"

"Eventually it goes into the Great Artesian Basin," said Charlotte with disgust.

"Exactly," said Barry.

"As someone who only recently arrived in this beautiful country,

I must say, I was shocked that this was even being considered, so I did some research."

Barry clicked on a number of slides, talking the class through them in his funny animated style:

BACKGROUND TO FRACKING IN AUSTRALIA
✓ Licences have been issued for tens of thousands of wells around Australia;
✓ More than 90% of people surveyed are against this practice;
✓ Mining Companies can use unlimited water but farmers have severe restrictions.

MEDIA SUPPORTS IT
✓ There have been some really big protests which the papers largely ignore;
✓ There are glossy ads in newspapers saying it's all ok;
✓ There are ads on television which even call it "clean energy".

GOVERNMENT SUPPORTS IT
✓ The Queensland Government was apparently originally told by its own experts that it's not worth the risk but they are doing it anyway;
✓ All governments support it because they need the money.

"The thing is," said Barry, "this is all speculation, we can find out the truth from other countries where it's been done already. My cousins back home live in a town where fracking has begun. Uncle Bob and Auntie Mary have a farm there, on the Fylde Coast, just north of Blackpool.

Let's see what they have to say. Barry switched on a recording of his uncle's voice, which was scratchy but quite loud through the speakers he had connected to his computer. Uncle Bob began to speak,

"We've had two earthquakes already, within five hundred metres of one of the wells and they still want to drill eight hundred wells over the next sixteen years. You know what?"

Uncle Bob was obviously very angry,

"The experts working for the drillers said the likelihood of 'fracking' setting off the earthquakes was less than .01%. How can they say that? They do the drilling and next thing we get the earthquakes. We've had two already and it's not like we get them all the time. Isn't it obvious? Do they expect us to prove that they caused them? Bloody experts, eh. Blimey."

"Maybe you guys should move down here," said Barry.

"Ah well Barry, here's the thing, now that we have been earmarked for drilling, we couldn't sell if we wanted to. Old Bill across the way, he has to sell and the agents have told him, his farm's not worth a cracker. Who's gonna buy it? It's just not fair."

There was a silence, Uncle Bob's voice was faltering and now it was obvious that he was too choked up to continue.

Crystal could see that some of the kids had tears in their eyes. Barry was choked up too as he stopped the recording. He was barely able to utter his conclusion to that segment.

"Now that's truth that is," he said grimly.

The students seemed quite moved and there was silence.

"You done real good Guvna," said Jay, in a cockney accent, trying to lighten the mood. A smile erupted across Hobbsy's face and he resumed his showman persona.

"But wait, there's more," he said, starting a clip from the movie

Gasland. "What they've done to Garfield County in Colorado has to be seen to be believed."

The class were shocked by the graphic footage of people lighting their tap water, and nobody could understand how laws designed to *protect water* had been changed so that they did not apply to fracking. They even interviewed a Government employee who openly spoke about how corrupt the approval process was. The whole thing was a massive disaster, although no doubt profitable for the drillers.

"And that my friends, is the story of fracking. They say there is no proof it causes damage, well, excuse me but it's just bullshit."

The crowd gave Barry a big cheer and Crystal let the swearing go. "Thank you Barry, that was really fantastic. The way you showed what's going on in Australia and then used the foreign evidence, it was really convincing. Well done, especially interviewing Uncle Bob." Crystal was delighted.

GASLAND

Barry was unaware that Jay had wanted to give him a taste of his own medicine and so had filmed parts of Barry's presentation, which was a good thing as it was very moving.

As everyone slowly made their way to lunch, Tina approached Crystal.

"Excuse me miss, can I talk to you for a minute."

"Of course," said Crystal.

"It's about Tommy," said Tina.

"What's up Tina," she asked, trying not to show any reaction.

"Well, he's a lawyer like dad, but he's not working at the moment. He's having some time off, partly he says, to find himself, and partly so he can help dad look after me. I was just wondering if you could give me Bradley's number. Do you think Bradley would mind?"

"I'm sure he'd be fine," said Crystal. "The other thing is, Bradley is a fantastic astrologer, and maybe he can help Tommy to find himself?"

"That's great," said Tina. "I don't have the details on me right now but if you give me Tommy's number, I will text them to him ok."

"That would be great Miss Stevens, thanks so much." "It's no trouble at all," said Crystal, happy to have the chance to contact Tommy.

Crystal sent Tommy a friendly text telling him Bradley's number and because she had a strong intuition to do so, she also mentioned he was a fabulous astrologer.

46

The Posters

Dane Capper set the triangle for a game of pool and then carefully lifted it, signalling to Jay that he could break. Jay lined up the white ball and expertly split the pack, sinking a ball immediately.

"I love this home ground advantage already," said his smiling doubles partner Barry Hobbs.

The boys were pleased that Jay had invited them back to his place after their double period of English was cancelled.

Jay sunk another ball, then Jacob missed and then Barry sunk one as well. He flashed another broad smile at his host and partner. Jay smiled back as Dane quickly assessed the chances of Barry's next shot. It was looking like a whitewash.

"No nudie runs ok," said Dane, well aware that on some pool tables when one team loses without sinking a ball, the other has to strip and run around the table.

Jacob didn't seem to be paying attention, even to the prospect of a nudie run. He was pretty quiet anyway, usually only speaking when he had something worthwhile to say. This appeared to be such a moment, as Jacob turned to Dane,

"I'm not fussed about the game, mate, I was just thinking about Teens for Truth. You know you have done a fantastic job, but....... well, Doug has the media in his pocket so we need to create our own publicity. Like, maybe we should just make thousands of posters and tell the real story, you know about the petition. Let's post them everywhere, how else can we make him care?"

"You are right, apart from money, publicity is all politicians seem to care about," said Dane, adding, "it's a great idea but who's going to put a thousand posters out Jacob?"

"Why not get each member to do their area," Jacob responded, "you know just a few telegraph poles near their house or something. If we spread that over all our members we could give Doug some nice true publicity."

Jacob was on a roll, probably pleased that everyone liked his suggestion. "Let's call it Where's Douggie?" he said. "You know, like *Where's Wally?* We could have a Facebook page or something."

"Doug will pee his paints," Jay said with a laugh.

"He deserves it after just ignoring us." Barry was also delighted.

"You are on fire Jacob," said Dane.

"Except for your pool playing which clearly needs some work." Barry couldn't resist rubbing it in and then he changed his tack. "Hey Dane, maybe you should send Doug's office an official letter, with the petition again, telling him how many signatures we have now. It might be useful down the track in case he tries to weasel out of it, you know, says he can't remember it or something."

"Good call Hobbsy, maybe we should do a letter about the fracking as well?" suggested Dane.

Jacob was on it again, "I can see it now, more posters with slogans like *Trust Doug to frack things up.*"

The boys all roared with laughter. Dane was delighted with this new inspiration. He really wanted to get the message across. He had no idea of just how serious things would get, why would he? He was just a kid playing pool with his mates.

47

Crystal's Dream

Crystal was so moved by Barry's talk that she had gone home and watched all of Gasland. It was astonishing to think that the American laws designed to keep water pure and clean had been amended to exclude fracking. 'Isn't that why they have such laws,' she thought?

"It really gets you thinking" said Beth who had watched it with her.

"I'm so proud of the kids. I could never have imagined how much they would get into all this stuff," said Crystal, unaware that she didn't really know the half of it.

She and Beth talked for a while and then she found herself yawning. She said goodnight to Beth and was soon fast asleep.

In her dream, she found herself in a beautiful forest running as fast as possible. She was being chased, but was not afraid. Rather, it was like a game and she was laughing as she ran.

Crystal felt connected to the forest as she stopped to hide behind a beautiful big old oak tree. She realised that the tree was laughing with her, and this felt perfectly natural in her dream.

"Ssshhhh," she said lovingly to the tree, "he'll hear us." Hiding behind the tree, both in silence as her playmate approached, Crystal knew he could sense her presence. She suddenly made her decision, turning to run again.

She ran through the forest as if floating on air and she could hear him laugh with delight as he chased her.

"I've got you now," he said.

He was far too quick and soon enough he was able to tackle her, bringing them both down gently in a velvety soft patch of clover. They lay on their backs looking up at the sun's rays filtering through the canopy of leaves and branches. Crystal was overcome by the beauty of this seemingly enchanted forest. Laying there together, in that moment, their two hearts beating as one, Crystal felt bliss that she had never felt before.

Later, walking through the forest they came upon a clearing and Crystal saw many people, all happily engaged in various activities. Some were tending exquisite gardens of vegetables and flowers, while others were happily engrossed in arts and crafts of some kind. She could sense their joy at just being absorbed in what they were doing. People greeted them with familiarity and open hearts as they breezed along together.

Crystal felt overwhelmed by her gratitude at being in such a magical place. Turning to smile at her beloved, she became aware for the first time that he was Tommy O'Brien.

She woke with quite a start.

48

Teenj gaining momentum

Things started to really get going over the next few weeks. The posters were an instant hit with the members of Teens for Truth. The idea spread like wildfire and the members placed them everywhere. There was no escape for Doug Toovey, particularly as Dane had followed Barry's suggestion and written a formal letter on behalf of the Group.

Where's Douggie, was a great success and posters were placed with great creativity. Jay stuck one on the bottom of one of his surfboards. He was savvy enough to know that his sponsors may not want to upset a politician, and so was only happy to do photos wearing a mask.

As it turned out, that made it even better. Jay was snapped soaring through the air in beautiful late afternoon light and a surfing magazine ran the shot as a full colour page. Doug's face was clearly visible along with the phrase *Poisoning our Water* and the magazine caption said, 'Phantom activist getting some air.'

Not to be outdone, Vanessa had her friends take a photo of her where she appeared to be naked behind the poster. Vanessa's and Jay's photos in particular were big hits and there were others, such as a collage of posters of Doug covering the back of a bus. They were now using posters of him in their fracking campaign. A lot of the adults were starting to pay attention as well.

Not long after Barry's presentation, the group had talked more about Uncle Bob, particularly the power of his words about his personal experience. Jacob suggested that they connect with other teens in places where fracking was happening. From there, the next step was to connect with teens in places where fluoride was still added to the water, or where that practice had recently been stopped.

They searched for stories on the internet and then through their membership links, they made contact with teenagers in those particular areas.

Jay also followed up the surfers who had spoken to Dane at the Presentation Party, who in turn put them in touch with teenagers in their towns. It wasn't long before they had quite a few members in the United Kingdom and America and some true life testimonials on the website.

At Albert's suggestion, the Group had told their members of a big gathering that was being held to raise community awareness about fracking. They wanted to get as many people there as possible, that way, it was more likely that they would get some publicity in the media.

49

Doug Returns

Doug Toovey had been invited to address the fracking rally by the concerned aboriginal elders and so timed his trip overseas to coincide with that date. When he returned his staff briefed him about the posters.

"Over a hundred posters of you, boss," his staff member, James Mitchell told him. They had initially tried to dismiss it as just some kids mucking around and they also did not want to spoil Doug's trip but now he was back, an explosive reaction was inevitable.

Mitchell initially tried to pull down the posters but they kept mysteriously reappearing so he gave up. He simply couldn't cope. He did take photos of some of the posters he had found. He scrolled through his IPhone and handed a typical image to Doug who studied it intently speaking out aloud as he read.

"Doug refused to simply watch a movie. Doug refused to accept a petition with over 400 signatures. Doug refused to explain about our water being poisoned." His voice increased in volume and pitch with each new refusal.

"How could they say this? Don't they know that I'm a man of the people." Doug was hurt and he seemed to have no memory of that day at the beach.

"Is Carol Jones behind this?" he asked angrily, acknowledging his main political rival.

"We think it's just the kids," said Mitchell.

"Mr Toovey, we also received this while you were away," said his secretary, Natalie Whitlock. She dared not say that her son was a member of Teens for Truth or that she thought the whole thing was actually funny. After all, he had acted like a weasel at the beach that day and it was unfair that the press made the kids look bad. From what she had heard, the kids had actually been quite polite.

She handed Doug a letter from Dane Capper. The letter politely reiterated the kids' concerns about the fluoride in the water and contained an updated copy of the Petition, noting that they now had over one thousand signatures. They also enclosed a copy of Firewater, and another movie called the Fluoride Deception.

Doug was livid. He had survived twenty years in Parliament by never allowing his name to be associated with negative publicity.

"We also received another letter from the kids," said Natalie. "Now they want to know about the fracking."

Doug's face went crimson, he knew that there was lots of money to be made from the fracking and it could not be jeopardized. Like fluoridation, that subject was also not negotiable. Natalie passed the letter to Doug. It was also from Dane Capper with another petition from the kids.

"Ok, I need some time to digest this." Doug motioned his staff towards his office door.

"Out," he screamed as if he needed to make himself even clearer. James Mitchell knew from experience to close it behind him as he left.

Doug dialled Felton Ross immediately. "How was the trip?" asked Felton pleasantly.

"How was the trip," mimicked Doug. "The trip was fine but that's not why I'm ringing, I'm ringing because there are posters of me all over the place, and I want to know what you are doing about it."

"It's a hard one boss, they are just kids. The usual methods don't apply."

THE FLUORIDE DECEPTION

What Felton meant was that the typical means of influencing adults, such as a little threat about losing their job, or their children, did not apply with kids.

"How are we supposed to scare the kids? Take their bikes away?" Felton was obviously uncertain about what to do.

"I don't care if it's different. I want this stopped .....stop this Dane Capper now," screamed Doug before slamming down the phone.

50

CRAIG and TINA's movie

Craig was delighted that Tina had insisted they film the rally against fracking, which they had attended on the weekend. It had given them the theme for their movie which was that the world would be a better place if people stood up together against the destruction of our planet. People could no longer sit back and let things get destroyed, they had to make a stand.

He and Tina interviewed as many people as they could, kids, adults and even the elderly.

"I've seen them do some really stupid things to make money," said one enraged pensioner, "but this really takes the cake. Their scientists say there's no proof that fracking will poison the water. No proof, they use toxic chemicals for goodness sake, doesn't anyone have common sense anymore?"

"What are they going to do," said another pensioner, "wait until the water is poisoned and then say, oh, now there's proof."

'At least the pensioners were able to laugh at the stupidity' thought Craig. He and Tina got some excellent interviews and footage of the gathering. It was unanimous, we are lucky to live on such a beautiful planet and we need to stand up *together* to the greedy people who only care about money.

They also spoke to some of the traditional people from the land about their idea of a Teenage Earth Day.

The elders were delighted, "Mother Earth will be happy that

you honour her," they had said. "Remember, your hearts hold the key to connecting with Mother Earth."

They had also said that the future of Earth is all about cooperation. "That is the way of nature, people need to learn from nature and work together like she does."

It was an amazing blessing for Tina and Craig to get this footage for their movie.

Craig could see Tina's joy as their project was taking shape. It was just the way her mother said. Many more people were now showing their love for the planet and it was uniting people of all shapes and sizes.

The elders also mentioned fear. "Do not let them trick you into being fearful in their world of time and money," they said, "your world will be created by what is in your hearts."

51

Tommy and Bradley

Tommy had struck up quite a friendship with Bradley Miller, who seemed pleased to be his spiritual mentor. Not only was he extremely knowledgeable about the ancient prophecies and wisdom, he was a strong believer that our society was carefully controlled so that people would not awaken to their true power.

"Newspapers, magazines and television make people feel like they need something outside themselves, like a new car, new clothes, or the latest electronic gadget. The advertisers wouldn't have it any other way." Bradley stopped and looked at Tommy,

"It doesn't matter what the item, the point is if you think you need anything outside of *self*, you won't be truly happy in your heart."

The media also makes people compare themselves with celebrities. I mean that's not going to make anyone happy is it. They foster *envy* and *comparison*, which are the enemies of a grateful heart.

The ancients knew that daily gratitude is a powerful way to bring abundance into their lives. This simple free tool is largely hidden to the modern world." Bradley was obviously very passionate but he was also very balanced as well.

"That's just what I say Tommy, you think about it for yourself. It's up to you what you feel," Bradley said wisely.

"Oh and Tommy," he added further, "please take my advice, if you do feel that things are as I say, please be gentle on those around you. Don't ram it down their throats, trust me, they may not be as open as you to hear this truth."

At Crystal's suggestion, Tommy had also asked Bradley about astrology.

"Astrology gets a bad rap because it's so misunderstood," said Bradley. "Think about it, the newspaper gives twelve different predictions each day, one for Aries, one for Gemini and so on. What say you're a Leo (which kind of freaked Tommy out as he was), well today, the paper might say that something lucky will happen to you. You and every other Leo? C'mon, that's like one twelfth of the world's population. It's ridiculous."

"When you put it that way, I can see what you mean," said Tommy, who sometimes read his horoscope and now wondered why he had never thought of that before.

"However," said Bradley enthusiastically, "used properly, astrology is an amazing science. Did you know that Benjamin Franklin used astrology to pick July 4, 1776 to sign the US Declaration of Independence? He chose that day because it was very powerful. There was a five planet eclipse that day. It's very easy to prove.

They even say a rich leader of society at that time bought a ticket for the Titanic but then decided not to go at the last minute. A number of his friends were quoted at the time saying that this was because of a meeting with his astrologer."

"You're kidding," said Tommy.

"No I'm not Tommy. The establishment tries so hard to discredit astrology and yet they use it themselves. I assure you, astrology can be an amazing tool for people to know themselves in great detail. Remember what Jesus said Tommy,

'The Kingdom of Heaven is within you and whosoever knoweth himself shall find it.'

Tommy said nothing, as he was simply processing all the information, and so Bradley continued,

"You should be able to find out the exact time of your birth either from your parents or the hospital. If you send me that information, I will prepare your own personal chart. I can show you your ultimate potential at birth and some of the challenges you must face to get there."

For some reason, Tommy thought of Crystal.

"I'd love that Bradley," he said gratefully. "Oh and one more thing," Tommy added, "do you really write down your dreams?"

"Of course," said Bradley, "you should try it."

He thanked Bradley for his time and made a commitment to really get to know himself. He really liked the idea of finding out his own unique gifts and challenges. Tommy knew that he was born in Sydney on 18 August 1986.

As he expected, his mum was able to locate the paperwork and within an hour of him calling her, she confirmed that Tommy was born at 5.55 am. Geez thought Tommy, maybe that's why I love watching the sunrise.

He arranged to see Bradley again and in the meantime, he read every self-help/spiritual book he could get his hands on.

52

Jasmine's friends

Another week had passed and Dane Capper had spent yet another Friday afternoon with Mike Waters and Craig Sceats. He was so passionate about Teens for Truth, it wasn't like work, it was fun and they were making great progress. He understood of course that Jay wanted to surf or skate every day, because he had to keep up his fitness as surfing would soon be his career.

Dane rode home as usual and as he reached his driveway he could hear the music blaring from the other side of the house. He knew that Simon had gone away for the weekend, 'it must be Jasmine and her university friends,' he thought, recalling her saying that a few of them were staying over tonight.

They are usually good for a laugh thought Dane so after showering and changing he headed over to the main part of the house. There was Jasmine, her boyfriend Steve, Phil and Jenny and another guy who Jasmine introduced as Kareem. He was some kind of shaman on a visit to Australia.

Jasmine had attended a talk he gave at the university, Energy Healing: A New Light on Ancient Techniques. They connected instantly and Kareem had been hanging out with her and her friends over the last few days. 'There is something different about him,' thought Dane, 'he is so calm and serene.'

The others all shook Dane's hand but when Kareem was

introduced he hugged Dane warmly and told him, "it is so good to meet you again, my brother." 'That's weird' thought Dane but he said nothing as Kareem seemed like a really pleasant guy.

They offered a beer to Dane but like Kareem, he politely declined. He was simply happy to sit on the couch and watch what they were watching. The computer was connected to his parents giant screen television and they were watching a mixture of music, comedy and spiritual movie clips, which they took turns to choose. Jasmine put on an old favourite, Love Shack by the B52's. She and Jenny had a great time dancing and singing and they seemed to know every single word.

The crew chatted happily, reviewing their week and debating the issues of the world. When Kareem's turn came he chose a clip of comedian Bill Hicks. "Hey. I know this guy," said Dane, "I've seen this, and it's so funny." The comedy skit was about magic mushrooms. Hicks telling his story of an experience he recently had:

"2 weeks ago my friends and I went to a ranch in Texas and took what has been described as a heroic dose of magic mushrooms. I'm glad they are against the law. You know what happened when I took them?

I lay in a field of green grass for 4 hours going my god, I love everything. The heavens parted, god looked down and reigned gifts of forgiveness onto my being. Healing me on every level, physically, emotionally and spiritually **and I realized our true nature is spirit not body, that we are eternal beings and that god's love is unconditional.** *There is nothing anyone can ever do to change that. It is only our illusion that we are separate from god or that we are alone.*

The reality is, we are one with god and he loves us."

Then with great sarcasm, in reference to the fact that these mushrooms are illegal, Hicks continued,

"Now if that isn't a hazard. I mean what's going to happen to the arms industry when we realize we are all one."

Hicks had himself and the audience in fits of laughter. It was great to see how much he was enjoying what would be his last performance as the cancer he was battling would finally take him two days later.

"They are trying to make unconditional love illegal?" joked Kareem.

"Oneness just isn't good for the economy you know," said Jasmine.

"The many indigenous tribes of South America have used such substances for as long as their records date," said Kareem. "It is a gift of nature, it crushes the perception of physical limitations, allowing the user to explore the world beyond the physical. It would help your Western Societies to see this."

"I agree," said Dane. "I thought he made the experience sound amazing, I wouldn't mind trying some of those mushrooms," he said to nobody in particular.

"Please do not attempt to go and eat mushrooms," said Kareem. "Some can be poisonous, you need the right kind prepared in the special way."

Phil shot Steve a quick glance, he seemed unsure what to say.

"How old are you Dane?" he asked, looking towards Jasmine. She knew exactly what Phil was thinking and quickly cut in,

"He's seventeen going on twenty seven, but he's still a baby... put it this way, he's still young enough that some things are better left unsaid."

Jasmine gave Phil a wink. It was obvious she was putting a stop to any thoughts he had of inviting Dane to tomorrow's ayahuasca ceremony, where they would be having an experience which was similar to the one Hicks described.

Dane hung out with the gang for quite a few hours and shared their meal. He liked their choice of film clips and their lively intellects. He particularly liked the clips that Kareem chose, which seemed to speak directly to him.

The one about the great planet alignment really had him thinking. There was really no other explanation for all of the ancients saying the same thing. They simply must have understood the cycles of the planets including the Great Central Sun which our sun and solar system revolves around. The mind boggles as to how the ancients had this information.

"This is a very significant time," said Kareem enthusiastically. "It is a great honour for any soul to be here on Earth at this time, the chance to evolve to a higher dimension other than by death."

While Jasmine and Jenny were making some coffee Dane excitedly told the boys about Teens for Truth, his trip to the police station, the posters and how they were really starting to put some pressure on the *establishment*. He obviously impressed them with his enthusiasm and daring.

"Hey Jas your brother is a maddog," yelled Steve affectionately.

Kareem listened quietly as they spoke and then finally, he said to Dane,

"My brother, it is wonderful that you see injustice and want change. I feel however that you are fighting the establishment. Tell me, are you and your brothers and sisters creating conflict or peace?"

Dane thought for a minute.

"I guess we are creating conflict in order to create peace. I mean, we have to let people know we want some changes but what we do ultimately want is a peaceful world."

Kareem looked at Dane and said patiently, "Conflict attracts conflict and peace attracts peace. That is the law of attraction, but of course, you already know this my brother. If you truly want peace, why not simply *be the change you want in the world.*

In other words, be peace and inspire all of your teens to do the same. Action created from a place of balance and harmony will be far more powerful, like the actions of Gandhi."

"Yeah," said Dane, "but you should see this guy Doug. He is a liar and we want everyone to know." Kareem seemed to stop and think and then attempted to relay his message in a way that Dane was more used to.

"I think it was George Carlin, another of your comedians who said something *like fighting for peace is like screwing for virginity,* he makes it so obvious, no?"

Dane appeared to be getting it and Kareem continued.

"You are here at this time to inspire many people Dane. I have seen this. It is important you see that peaceful change is what is needed. This man Doug, all these things you speak of, they are all a part of you, everything is connected and you are best to change these things by peaceful means rather than by conflict. Each of you could hold the space of a peaceful New Earth within yourselves."

Dane looked a little confused so Kareem continued. "You've done this before you know, in other times and places. Trust me. If you sit still and ponder on this, you will feel the truth of my words."

He looked right at Dane. "You have the heart of a lion but you also need the wisdom of an owl. Remember, the great alignment is coming soon."

Dane was moved by Kareem's words but he did not know what to say, "wow thanks for that," was all he could manage.

They stayed up talking and laughing well after Dane had crashed. At some point, Steve and Phil told Jasmine they thought Dane was probably old enough for the ayahuasca ceremony.

"Think about it Jas, he is leading all these teenagers, he really needs the wisdom," said Phil. As Jasmine thought about this Kareem had the final say,

"Dane must experience the wisdom of the ceremony."

53

Invitation to Ayahuasca

The next morning Jasmine told Dane, "we are going to an ayahuasca ceremony tonight. It's much like the mushrooms in the Bill Hicks skit. We talked about it baby bro and we think you are mature enough to come along. In fact," Jasmine added, "Kareem virtually insisted that we take you."

"Are you gonna get me stoned on mushrooms sis?" asked Dane.

Jasmine's reply was serious, "Dane, this is not a game, so you must treat it with reverence. Ayahuasca is actually a sacred experience that has been used by wisdom seekers for eons to break through physical limitations. It just gets bad publicity nowadays, like everything else that helps wisdom and empowerment."

"I think you are mature enough," she continued, "because you are a very special and unusual seventeen year old. I am ok with you doing it, but it's your call. If you do participate, you will have to do so with maturity and reverence like all of us. You will need to set a *sacred intention* for your journey.

As I said, it was actually Kareem who insisted you participate. He said you will carry the wisdom to your generation, which seems a tad dramatic to me, but he is coming with us too, so he can mentor you. Kareem has done this many times before."

"Sounds like a plan," said Dane, smiling broadly, remembering Bill Hicks' words:

I lay in a field of green grass for four hours going My God, I love everything.

'I hope that happens to me,' he thought.

54

Tommy's Reading

Bradley agreed to do Tommy's astrology reading at his house on Saturday morning. Tommy drove over full of anticipation and he wasn't disappointed. "Service or suffering," was the first thing Bradley said, as if this was obvious from the complicated diagram on his desk.

"All I know is that I'm a Leo," said Tommy staring back blankly. "You might need to explain it a bit more."

There was a large circle divided into 12 portions, which Bradley explained were houses. "These symbols around the outside of the circle are signs, representing star constellations," he said, "and the ones inside the circle are planets. See this symbol here is Leo, and this red circle is the sun, so as you rightly point out Tommy, your sun is in Leo. There is however so much more to it than that," Bradley said enigmatically.

"This picture depicts what you would have seen in the sky had you been outside looking up when you took your first breath. Your unique energy is a function of the location of the planets and star constellations at that precise moment. They all emit their own special energy. These are the ingredients in your cake mix. How you choose to bake it is up to you."

Tommy simply stared at the diagram.

"It's quite obvious Tommy, you are someone who is here to help the helpless and downtrodden. Just to be clear, this doesn't mean you *will* do this. It means that you *can* do this and what's more, that you will probably be happiest if this is your journey.

Like you, Abraham Lincoln was born with Jupiter in Pisces and he wrote of his great compassion for the slaves in America before he became President. This placement shows great vision. Another who had it was Leonardo da Vinci?"

Bradley talked as Tommy wrote. "I'm glad you are taking a break to find yourself Tommy, you really could be here to benefit humankind. Of course, Jupiter in Pisces is just one element, there are many others which may, or may not, compliment this. You have Saturn in the fourth house, which also suggests that you have a karmic role to play for the greater good of humanity.

With your sun in Leo and with a Leo ascendant as well, you have strong leadership potential. Spirituality and leadership is a wonderful combination."

Tommy explained to Bradley that he was actually a lawyer but his career was on hold.

"On reflection, I wasn't totally comfortable serving large corporations," said Tommy, as if already influenced by what he had heard.

"Obviously," said Bradley.

It wasn't all good either. As Tommy reflected on the astrologer's lofty words, Bradley looked up thoughtfully,

"Oh and Tommy, be very careful, I'm guessing you have a certain way with the ladies and that this can sometimes get you into trouble?"

Tommy's embarrassed smile was all the answer Bradley needed.

"Venus in Libra," he said by way of explanation. After some further study of the chart, he really blew Tommy away.

"You may have had such an incident recently, perhaps this is why you are now trying to find yourself? The recent transit of Saturn suggests this possibility."

Tommy could not believe what he'd heard. He started to tell the story about Heidi the summer student at his old law firm.

Bradley put up his hand to stop him, "it's your lesson Tommy, not mine."

Later, after thinking about it all day, Tommy was convinced that the whole thing with Elliott and his luck with the trading was part of some bigger picture.

THE CIRCLE OF LIFE

Lying in bed that night he felt happy he could be of service. He just hoped that Crystal would somehow be involved.

The next morning Tommy remembered that he had dreamt about Elliott and luckily, he had kept a pen and paper by his bed. He could vaguely remember them talking, Elliott continuing with his wise, otherworldly persona. Tommy had been listening, and then he had scribbled something down in the dead of night.

He quickly reached to see what he had written.

Crystal will seek your help soon.

55

Ayahua∫ca Ceremony

By mid-afternoon on Saturday, Jasmine and Dane and the others were packed and ready for the drive to Ravenswood. They were excited about the ceremony and spoke about it as they went. They stopped to collect Kareem on the way and eventually found the ceremony headquarters which were perched on a secluded hilltop surrounded by beautiful gardens.

They brought their things into the ceremony hall and were given a page of instructions. Each of them then walked outside and stood barefoot on the Earth, to connect and plant their intentions for the ceremony.

Kareem had entertained Dane and the others during the car trip with incredible stories of his past experiences. Eventually Dane decided on his intention as simply *to see the truth*.

Those present sat around the outside of a large circle. Each had ample cushions and pillows and could set themselves up comfortably for *the journey*. Kareem was able to tell Dane lots of stuff in the car but now it was just him. The journey is an intensely personal experience and talking for any reason is discouraged. Dane felt the butterflies in his stomach and went to the bathroom twice before they started.

Once everyone was ready, a man in the centre in a monk like robe made the introduction. It was done with great reverence.

Dane felt more relaxed as he listened to the words and the beautiful music that was playing. They went around the circle each taking a turn going into the centre and drinking a small cup of foul tasting greyish liquid.

'Yuk,' he thought, barely managing to not spew it back up. As the soft music played in the background he settled back into his cushions with a bucket by his side just in case.

He sat totally still, feeling very comfortable. His body was feeling heavier by the second. Eventually it was as if he had no body.

At one point, Dane noticed that Phil was tipping over. Still seated, still upright, just tipping over in slow motion without even trying to cushion his fall. Everyone heard the thud as Phil literally tipped over onto the floor.

The thing was, nobody could move. Dane felt as if he was in quicksand. After what seemed like eons, two of the organizers made it to Phil. He was still sitting, just tipped over, that's all. They checked to see that he was conscious, then brought him back up and adjusted his cushions and Phil continued as if nothing had happened.

'E-v-e-r-y-t-h-i-n-g i-s f-i-n-e,' thought Dane.

Dane's cushions simply melted into his body, he saw his life, people he knew, Jay, Vanessa, Jacob, Miss Stevens, his parents, everybody. He saw his faithful family dog Blackie. He could even feel how much Blackie loved him.

"All life is light," said Dane. Well he wasn't actually talking, it was just that in his ayahuasca state, Dane could talk without talking. He could also walk without walking. In fact, he could even fly without flying.

As Kareem had said, he was now beyond the boundary of physical limitations. He was the movie maker of his own script.

As time stood still, Dane could feel the microscopic pulsations of the very cosmos itself. He could feel waves of energy, waves of love.

A butterfly darted back and forth and then perched on Dane's arm. The butterfly was the Divine Creator. It looked at Dane and told him telepathically we are one.

Dane's arm and the butterfly then became waves of light which eventually fused together.

This was Dane's realization of oneness. He thought again about what Bill Hicks had said during his last performance,

"It is only our illusion that we are separate from god or that we are alone."

Dane now understood this and as he did, he saw the waves of love extend all across the universe. Love is the cosmic glue for everything. He could place himself into or out of the illusion at will. In...out, in...out. He saw that he was the creator of his experience.

He saw Albert and he understood that they had roamed the outback together in a life gone by.

He now understood Kareem's wisdom. They should not be in conflict with the *few*, for conflict itself is a vibration of the illusion, a vibration of the ego. They could only effect real change from a vibration of love. We must be the change we want in the world. Peaceful change. He had lived this wisdom in lives gone by. It was just as Kareem had said.

Dane saw teenagers everywhere, avoiding the conflict which he felt that those in authority wanted. They were acting out peaceful change, as the people of India had done in the time of Gandhi. He knew that all conflict must be avoided.

Dane also saw himself lying on a bed in a hospital. Was he alive or was he dead? He wasn't sure, he was just observing himself from afar. He felt that he had a choice. It was not a choice between life and death although that is how it would appear to most people.

It was a choice between *truth* and *illusion*. He saw that his choice was like the choice which mankind now faced.

Dane sat still, hour after hour, blissfully travelling all over the Universe. Neither time nor space, were boundaries for his consciousness.

After four or five hours, he was vaguely aware that there was a second drink available for those who wished. He declined, he was fine, and probably could not have moved anyway. He continued his travels for a few more hours and then eventually, he fell asleep.

The next morning some of those present recounted their experiences. Dane enjoyed listening although he did not say anything himself other than,

"I asked to see the truth and I was shown that everything is love and we are all one."

As for the details, his experience was too great for mere words to describe.

Jenny's description of her experience was profound. She had asked to see her mother who had died when she was quite young. Tearfully, she told of how she saw beautiful scenes of nature and was told by the voice of her birth mother, that the *Earth is your mother, you are never alone.*

"This is what the indigenous people tell their children," said Kareem. "That way, they are never apart from their mother's love."

Yet again, Dane was moved by the profound wisdom of the indigenous people and he wondered again why it was not adopted by our society at large.

When Dane returned home, he went straight to his room and sat in stillness and silence. He experienced a feeling of harmony beyond anything he had ever known. He remembered the class where they talked about the world being a hologram and how Mike gave the example of a rose. If you cut off a small part of the hologram and magnified it, you would see the whole of the rose within that small part.

In effect, we contain everything within us. He understood now that Teens for Truth would be most effective by simply creating or encouraging the changes we want in the world within every member, peacefully, and then together creating a new world. Creating balance from a place of balance.

For some reason, he felt compelled to record his thoughts so he set up his video camera and off he went. He burnt a copy onto a disc which he labelled *Teens for Truth: Way of Peace.*

"That afternoon, Dane posted an update on the Teens for Truth website. *"The only thing that is real is love. Everything else is an illusion."*

Felton Ross read these words and a rye smile etched across his face

"My dear boy, we can't let you keep on saying that, somebody might start to believe you. Somebody could get hurt." He laughed his maniacal laugh.

56

General studies: Lance talks about Drugs

Crystal introduced Lance Halloran, who thought that the world would be a much better place if everybody was allowed to take responsibility for their own health.

"As I will explain to you," said Lance, "much of our health industry has a big conflict of interest between *their profits* and *your health*. Big business is always talking about how wonderful things are and how wonderful all their products are. The reality however is that people are sicker and unhappier than ever. Lance paused to let his point sink in and then, after a furtive glance around the room, he continued seriously.

I have been on anti-depressants." Lance made his confession to the class, much like a participant in an Alcoholics Anonymous group.

"I know firsthand about the powerful side effects. We have heard about fluoridation, which is medication without consent. Well, what about medication *with* our consent and our parent's consent? What about the *legal* drugging of our youth?"

'What a powerful and personal way to start his presentation,' thought Crystal.

Lance showed a clip of a lady named Gwen Olsen. Ms Olsen was an *industry insider* with fifteen years of executive experience in the pharmaceutical industry. She recently confessed the obvious in a widely viewed film clip, namely, that for pharmaceutical companies, 'curing customers is bad for business.'

She confirmed that the pharmaceutical industry is really all about *disease maintenance and symptom management.*

"It's kind of obvious when you think about it," said Lance, "but it's still shocking when you actually hear it from an industry insider."

GWEN OLSEN

Lance quoted statistics from a book called 'The Truth about Drug Companies' by Dr. Marcia Angell, a former editor in chief of the New England Journal of Medicine.

> "In 2002, the combined profits for the ten drug companies in the Fortune 500 *(kind of like the biggest US Companies)* were $35.9 billion."

"Can you believe this?

> Dr Angell described the pharmaceutical industry as *'primarily a marketing machine to sell drugs of dubious benefit.'*

And they have our trust. It's so wrong!"

His nostrils flared. Crystal could feel his passion as he posed another obvious question. "Why are these companies making so much money when they are really **just managing symptoms and maintaining disease?**" said Lance.

"Because we let them" said Hobbsy as if just realising this for the first time.

Lance ran a clip of a TV news story about Danny Gyles, a twenty two year old who had been on Ritalin since he was diagnosed with attention deficit hyperactive disorder (ADHD) at the age of four.

"That's right, they have been dumbing him down with his daily dose since he was four. That's eighty percent of his life on Ritalin," Lance was obviously disgusted.

THE TRUTH ABOUT DRUG COMPANIES

"According to Gyles, the doctors just kept on giving him repeat prescriptions. When it eventually became obvious to him that nobody was actually monitoring his medication, he decided to simply stop taking it and document it in a movie. Danny described the experience as follows,

> *"Although it was very challenging at first, four months later, I have never felt better, I have gained over ten kilos and am sleeping better than ever."*

Danny then told of other long term Ritalin users with similar experiences. They were also featured in his movie.

"Wow," said Lance, "it's almost like they missed their childhood, they were zombies instead of kids. Put up your hand if you think it's shocking that Danny had to work this out for himself."

Every student raised their hand and so did Crystal.

Lance seemed to enjoy this and did it again.

"Put your hand up if you've watched Thrive?"

Half of those in the room raised their hands, including Crystal.

"I'll tell you what," said Lance enthusiastically, "this next story shows just how spot on *Thrive* is. There is a segment where Kimberly Gamble talks about the health system and how cancer has run through her family like a raging river. Her main point was, 'It's all about the patents.' The first time I watched it, I didn't understand this, but now I do.

What she was saying is that if a drug cannot be patented, it won't be part of the system. The reason is simple, it won't be as profitable for the drug companies if they don't own a patent to ensure the drug is theirs alone to sell.

This next story shows how true that is, for even the most effective drugs."

Lance clicked on a slide which showed a book cover,

A REMARKABLE MEDICINE HAS BEEN OVERLOOKED
By Jack Dreyfus

"Jack Dreyfus was a very successful American known as the Lion of Wall Street. Despite his wealth, Mr Dreyfus was depressed and saw a psychiatrist six days a week for over four years. This was no ordinary man, and on his own hunch, he asked his doctor if he could try a drug given to epileptics called phenytoin (PHT and also known as Dilantin). He read that this drug could regulate the body's electrical circuits and he just had a sudden hunch about his depression.

His doctor agreed and he was immediately cured by PHT, something that more than one thousand visits to his psychiatrist had not achieved.

He then recommended PHT to other people he knew who had depression. They also obtained prescriptions and they were cured too.

Being a kind, pragmatic and community minded man, Jack Dreyfus wanted as many depression sufferers as possible to get this drug. He tried for the next forty years to arrange for this drug to be widely available for the American people. This meant PHT had to be added to the list that doctors use when they are prescribing drugs. Mr Dreyfus created and funded his own Medical Foundation, which conducted a vast number of studies on PHT. He even met with two American Presidents to get support right from the top.

So what was the problem? According to his extensive research, PHT was widely effective, cheap and not habit forming.

The problem, was that PHT was cheap because it was 'invented' a long time ago and then rediscovered many years later after the patent had expired. Sure it might be a very effective drug but without a patent, it had far less commercial value.

Jack Dreyfus wrote numerous books about this experience including *A Remarkable Medicine has been Overlooked,* and his final book before his death which was titled, *Written in Frustration.*

"Here is the book," said Lance angrily, "you can probably work out from the title how he went."

He waved the book as he spoke and he showed everyone a picture of the twenty three thousand studies in medical journals, all in a pile.

"Look at all those folders," Lance said angrily.

"Jack Dreyfus was unable to succeed, and he called this a great injustice, questioning whether the US Food and Drug Administration (FDA), which had blocked him all those years, was really for the benefit of the public, or the drug companies. How disappointing it must have been to him that after such a long campaign, Americans (like Australians), still are not able to utilise or benefit from this drug.

It should at least please him that PHT is now widely used in China, Russia, India, Mexico and Ghana."

Crystal was impressed by the real examples that Lance had come up with. The kids all passed around Lance's copy of 'Written in Frustration,' and looked at the photos of the many studies.

"This just makes me so angry," said Lance, and the class sympathised with him. Everyone, except for Dane, that is.

Ever since his *awakening* on Saturday night, Dane saw the

world a little differently. He felt peaceful and harmonious. Like an Ascended Master, he accepted that everything happened for a reason in accordance with some higher plan. As we are all one, any conflict is pointless.

WRITTEN IN FRUSTRATION

"There is no point being angry Lance," he said wisely. "These people are the ones that need the greatest healing. Rather than fight with the FDA and the pharmaceutical companies, people should just resolve to take responsibility for their own health, just like Danny Gyles. If everyone did that, then the problems would gradually disappear."

Nobody said anything so Dane kept going, speaking like a guru delivering a sermon to a group of followers. Even Crystal was enthralled.

"People like to give away their power because this is what our society teaches. Take back your power and create peaceful change. As you do this, you are subconsciously giving others permission to do the same by your example.

Also, don't get too hung up on the negatives. What about all the positives from the movie Thrive," Dane added, "like the messages from the ancients, and in the crop circles, making it clear that we are not alone and giving us hints that free energy really does exist.

Everything really depends on raising the collective consciousness.

Current methods of getting energy involve combustion, exploding things, tearing things apart, and of course, a great deal of greed. These all stem from a consciousness of conflict.

When a critical mass of us become harmonious, extracting

energy from the environment harmoniously will seem like the only real choice and it will happen with ease and grace."

"Wow, Dane seems really different,' thought Crystal.

His words made sense, but they also puzzled the other kids, especially Lance. He was expecting Dane to embrace this medication issue as part of the Teens for Truth movement.

In a way, Dane was speaking to them just like Kareem had spoken to him. That was not even a week ago, and yet, it seemed like a lifetime. Dane knew the other kids would get this at the right time.

At lunchtime, Dane gave Jay a disc for safekeeping. "This is the truth," he said, "it's very important, please keep it…just in case anything should happen."

"What do you mean just in case?" asked Jay, appearing puzzled.

"It's nothing to worry about ok, just promise me you'll keep it safe," said Dane.

Dane was clearly acting a little weird, especially when he kept stressing the importance of Jay keeping the disc safe. Jay had actually wanted to talk with Dane about something else. While Dane was off having his guru awakening, *something* had happened between Jay and Vanessa, and it was playing on Jay's mind.

It obviously wasn't the right time to talk to Dane about it so Jay kept it quiet for now.

THE 100TH MONKEY SYNDROME

57

Simon's Little Bingle

Simon heard a bang and felt his car get pushed forward. He jumped out to investigate. It wasn't serious, just inconvenient. Someone had rammed into the back of his car. The lady driving the other car was very apologetic and also very attractive. Simon knew he was obliged to call the police but he felt no need. Jennifer Jones was obviously honest.

They had a lovely chat while she wrote down her details for him and she ended up offering to take Simon out to dinner that night to make it up to him for the damage.

"Yes, tonight. It's the least I can do," she said kindly. He had no plans for the evening and just had to leave a message for Dane to let him know he wouldn't be home. Not that Dane would care, today was his gym afternoon and he usually came home exhausted, ate dinner and crashed. He would remind Dane that he could have all of last night's leftovers, he would definitely be happy about that.

All in all, Simon was quite chuffed to have been asked out by such an enchanting woman. 'What a way to meet a gorgeous lady?' he thought. Who cares about the small bump in the rear of his car?

58

TINA'ſ IDEA ABOUT THE NATURE ƧPIRITƧ

Craig was incredibly excited when Tina told him the Findhorn story and her idea about incorporating reconciliation with the nature spirits, into the Teenage Earth Day.

He had gone straight to the library and found a book about Findhorn. The book confirmed everything Ivy had said. Through faith and their guidance from the spirit world, a few hardy souls had established a Garden of Eden on a barren windswept area in the north of Scotland. Craig knew that this defied all logic and reason.

There was lots of hard work, of course, but the main reason they created a miracle was that they were being assisted by the nature spirits.

Craig was amazed to read in great detail about the heirachy of beings who assisted with Findhorn including devas who crafted the energetic blueprint for each plant and elementals, such as gnomes and fairies, who used those blueprints to build up the plant form. Obtaining communications from the devas required great sensitivity, stillness and reverence because those beings are far more sensitive than humans.

Craig has a genius I.Q. and is able to rapidly digest information. The more he read about this, the more he wondered why it wasn't a simple solution to the world's food and farming problems?

The book explained that the nature spirits were here to help us tend the garden. That was their purpose for being here. They felt great sorrow that modern man refused to believe in their existence or ask for their help. The story was obviously true because their amazing farming results in such a difficult environment spoke for themselves and baffled industry observers.

Today, Findhorn is a very well established institution with a track record of growing massive fruits and vegetables. The whole story was fascinating to Craig. The book had lots of quotes from Pan, the mighty head of the Elementals and Nature Spirits. One quote in particular gave Craig his answer:

> *"I [Pan]am the servant of Almighty God, and I and my subjects are willing to come to the aid of mankind, in spite of the way he has treated us and abused nature, if he affirms his belief in us and asks for our help."*

Craig borrowed the book and called Tina. He was excited and had to meet and tell her face to face.

"You are right Tina, the world needs to know about this, urgently. The Nature Spirits are a wonderful resource and they truly want to come to our aid. I agree, let's all affirm our belief and ask the nature spirits for help as part of our movie and Teenage Earth Day."

Tina grabbed Craig and gave him the biggest hug.

59

Felton Ross

Felton Ross had spent the past few weeks watching Dane Capper and studying his movements. He couldn't sabotage Dane's car for example, because he didn't drive. Some of Dane's friends drove but Felton knew from experience that friends could make things messy. He did not like too many variables on a job.

Dane's parents were away, which was a big plus. His sister was rarely home during the week, also a big plus. The main problem was that his older brother was around a lot. He didn't seem to have a girlfriend or much of a social life. Felton was confident he could create an appropriate diversion for him, at the right time. The other variable was the family Labrador. Felton knew from experience that a nice piece of fillet steak laced with a strong sedative would easily take care of the dog.

Felton had formulated a plan about how he wanted to do things. He knew that Dane went to the gym with his mates on Tuesday afternoons. That would be his best chance and so he arranged a lovely distraction for Simon.

When Tuesday arrived, he had everything organised. After Dane left for gym, he entered Dane's house through the adjoining bushland, finding the kitchen where he had observed Dane with his binoculars. He knew Dane's habits well and was confident he would return home from the gym around 8 pm, heat up last night's leftovers, drink at least one jug of cold water and then retire to his room. He did what he had to do and then left.

Everything had gone according to plan until he received Jennifer's text, 'our friend insisted on leaving, he's on his way now, sorry.'

Simon had decided to come home early, something about Jennifer was not right. Initially, he was flattered when she offered to buy him dinner but why would a girl that beautiful be so insistent that he come back to her place on their first date? He was mulling that very issue over in his mind as she tried her hardest to persuade him.

"C'mon Simon, you won't regret it," she said smiling seductively. He was also thinking about something Jennifer had said earlier, he was certain that she had contradicted herself. It made the hairs on the back of his neck stand up and gave him a bad feeling in his stomach.

When he finally escaped her clutches, he drove home quickly. His suspicions were aroused even further when their faithful family dog Blackie failed to meet him, as he hopped out of his car in the driveway.

He rushed into Dane's room and was initially relieved to see him safely at home and fast asleep. Simon still felt that something wasn't right. He turned on the light and immediately noticed traces of foam around Dane's mouth. He was unconscious. Simon frantically called for an ambulance.

Within the hour, Dane was in the hospital bed he had seen in his vision, symbolically balanced between life and death, like so many aspects of our modern world.

60

Crystal

First thing the following morning, Crystal was called into Trevor Rawles' office.

"Good Morning Miss Stevens, please have a seat."

Rawles manner was polite but he seemed cold and a little standoffish to Crystal.

She was already aware that Rawles was disliked by the other teachers and did not get involved in day to day teaching issues. To add to her confusion, John Williams, the English Master, was also present.

"I'll get straight to the point Miss Stevens; we have had a number of complaints about you. It seems you have been inciting your Year 11 students into, shall we say, rebellious behaviour. A number of teachers and parents, prominent Parents & Citizens Committee Members in fact, have made complaints about your teaching style." Rawles was dispassionate.

"Inciting rebellious behaviour?" Crystal almost spat the words from her mouth, such was their distastefulness.

"I'm sorry Trevor, I have no idea what you mean. In fact, I have actually had great feedback from my students." Crystal was genuinely mystified. She looked at Williams for support but he said nothing and by his body language, it seemed that he did not wish to get involved.

"Well, for example," countered Rawles, "for the Year 11 economics essay on globalisation, a number of students said it was actually a *bad* thing. That is not their syllabus. One student wrote that globalisation 'is *a totally bogus lie designed to give market power to large corporations,'* and that *'it's funded largely with Government subsidies.'* He cited among other things, a movie called 'The Economics of Happiness.' I understand that you mentioned this movie in your class."

THE ECONOMICS OF HAPPINESS

Crystal felt quite defensive, 'what is wrong with teaching kids to think for themselves' she thought. Her words were more conciliatory.

"Trevor, I think it's pretty well accepted that globalisation has caused various problems, and anyway, isn't it up to the kids to put forward their own opinions in their essays? I have taught my students to be balanced in their research and I assume that the assignments in question were well researched."

"That's not the point Miss Stevens. We have also had complaints by a prominent parent, a doctor no less, that you have been questioning our medical system. I hardly think it's your place to do this."

"Again Trevor, I showed a clip from 'Simply Raw', as an illustration of an interesting experiment with diabetics. The children loved it and, well, the results in that movie speak for themselves.

Another student referred to 'Forks over Knives', in her assignment. She sourced that movie herself and I actually learned a lot from it. I learnt from her. The study in that movie was called the most comprehensive study ever undertaken of the relationship between diet and the risk of disease, by no less than the New York Times and the findings were very clear. It is a very significant study Trevor."

"Nevertheless, those views are not necessarily accepted by our society. We as a school must stick to certain,.....well, what I mean is, that it's not up to us to create a generation of rebels, questioning their parents."

"Rebels no, I agree Trevor, but independent thinkers, yes," countered Crystal, still holding her ground.

"As I have said Miss Stevens, I have heard from a number of sources that you encouraged your students to watch these kinds of videos. We consider this to be inappropriate behaviour and accordingly, the school is suspending you immediately until further notice."

Crystal was shocked. She looked at John Williams, who shrugged his shoulders weakly. She wanted to argue, to find out more details, but she was so devastated that she couldn't even speak.

"Don't worry Miss Stevens, proper arrangements will be made for your classes. We would like you to leave the school grounds immediately and we request that you do not contact any of your students."

Minutes later, Crystal was making the sad and lonely 'walk of shame' to the school car park, carrying a box of her belongings.

As she was driving out of the school, she suddenly thought of Tommy. She knew he was a lawyer. Maybe he might be able to offer her some advice?

She pulled over and dialled his number and was relieved to hear him answer.

"Tommy, it's Crystal Stevens, can you meet me? I've been suspended from my job. I..." Crystal started to cry.

"Hey, it's OK Crystal," he said in a soothing voice, which immediately made her feel a little better.

"Do you know Cafe Destiny?" he asked, knowing full well that she did, and that this was the moment he had dreamt of.

I hope you enjoyed reading The Awakening enough to want to help spread this story by word of mouth, which is the way of nature.

If you would like to share the first six chapters of **The Awakening** with a friend or friends, please email them this link…

 or go to:
www.itsourearthtoo.com.au/pages/book-preview

How about a reminder of the release of Book 2 'The Gathering' If you would like this please scan here…

 or go to www.itsourearthtoo.com.au/pages/join-us

The Awakening is also available in E Book and Audio formats. We hope you will join the **It's Our Earth Too Community.** To see our website or like us on Facebook please scan here…

 or go to www.itsourearthtoo.com.au

I am interested to hear what you have to say so feel free to send me a message at itsourearthtoo@gmail.com

David Still

Printed in Australia
AUOC02n1028140616
276581AU00002B/2/P